BELLA'S VINEYARD

Bella Tennyson is a stranger in a strange land. She and her gambling addict brother have travelled to America to claim a vineyard left to them by their aunt, also called Bella. When Bella and Andrew are threatened by local big shot, Arthur Griffiths, it seems their only friends are the handsome part-Cherokee marshal, Vance Eagleson, and May Tucker, the loyal friend of their late aunt. As tensions rise in an unforgiving land, Bella and Vance fall in love . . .

Books by Sally Quilford
in the Linford Romance Library:

THE SECRET OF HELENA'S BAY

SALLY QUILFORD

BELLA'S VINEYARD

Complete and Unabridged

LINFORD
Leicester

First published in Great Britain in 2010

First Linford Edition
published 2011

British Library CIP Data

Quilford, Sally.
    Bella's vineyard. - -
    (Linford romance library)
    1. Love stories.
    2. Large type books.
    I. Title II. Series
    823.9'2–dc22

    ISBN 978–1–4448–0741–7

Printed and bound in Great Britain by
T. J. International Ltd., Padstow, Cornwall

This book is printed on acid-free paper

1

Bella Tennyson began to think their travels would never end. A long sea journey, several stagecoaches, the Trans-Continental Railway, and more stagecoaches had left her body in a permanent state of motion. Even on the nights they stopped in hotels, and she was able to put her head on a pillow after a long day's travel, she fancied she heard the horses' hooves and it seemed the bed underneath her rolled as much as the coach.

'It won't be long now, Bella,' said Andrew as they began the final leg of their journey.

Outside the coach window, the vast country spread before them. Bella had come from a small town in the middle of England, and it had never taken more than a day to travel to the coast by train. This new world just kept on going. *It must end soon*, she thought.

True, the landscape was beautiful, and the sheer scale had taken her breath away to begin with. But after all the travel, through wind and rain, then heat and dust, she prayed for the land to come to an end somewhere.

An Englishman travelling on the railway, who had lived in America for many years, had told them, 'Men can go mad in this country, with all this space to play with. It does something to their mind. The land you're going to is lawless. That's what comes of being so far from civilisation. If you don't mind me saying so, Sir,' the man turned to Andrew, 'it's a bad idea to take this young lady out to California. Take her back to New York.'

Andrew had given Bella the guilty look he wore almost as a mask since they left England.

'We will endure,' he said.

Bella had nodded. Instead of enduring, she could be at home, rather than being thousands of miles from all that she had known for twenty-two years.

She looked, without really seeing, out of the coach window. There was no end in sight. She suppressed a silent scream. Yes, she might well go mad here, but she feared more for her brother's sanity.

The men sitting opposite them in the coach did not help her state of mind. They wore the large brimmed hats that were common to the country, with thick, double-breasted coats and stove-pipe chaps. Their hats were lined with sweat and the coats stained with gravy and all manner of foodstuffs. Every now and then they drank from a shared bottle of sour-smelling alcohol, an aroma like nothing Bella had ever known. To make matters worse, they chewed tobacco and then spat it out of the window — not always into the wind — whilst on the wall behind them, the coach regulations forbade such behaviour.

Bella wished Andrew would say something, but understood why he didn't. The large guns at the men's hips were enough to silence anyone.

In the far corner of the coach, a man dressed in a long, black coat leaned back, with his hat pulled down over his face. His long, muscular legs were barely able to stretch the length of the coach, whilst a tanned hand rested on the open window. She had no idea if he was awake or asleep. Sometimes, and with no real reason to believe it, she sensed he was listening. His stillness unnerved her. It didn't seem natural compared to her disturbed equilibrium. He had been that way since Bella and Andrew boarded the coach. The two men chewing tobacco had at least raised their hats to her. It seemed that their manners extended no further.

'What do you think he'll be like?' one of the men said. He was the smaller of the two, with bright red hair and the beginnings of a pot belly. Bella guessed he was about twenty-five years old.

'Don't matter,' said the other man. He was heavily set, and could have been anywhere between the ages of forty and fifty. When he took his hat off to Bella, he revealed that the hair that had stuck out of the bottom was all that he had. 'He ain't gonna live much longer than the last marshal.'

'I hear he's a college boy. Got degrees and everything.'

'I hear his great-grandpappy was a Cherokee. Ain't no amount of college gonna wash that dirt off a man's skin,' said the big man, punctuating the comment by spitting on the floor.

'Excuse me.' The words came from Bella's mouth as a croak. She coughed a little, partly to clear her throat and partly to stem the tide of nausea. 'Excuse me, Sir, but the sign says that you're supposed to spit into the wind outside the coach, and I would be very grateful if you did.'

Andrew put his hand on his sister's arm, to signal her to halt her breathless tide of words.

'Well, well,' said the big man. 'What do you think of that, Tom?' He turned to his friend. 'The sign says we're supposed to spit into the wind.'

'I don't know about that, Bill, but then I ain't never learned to read.' Tom spat onto the floor of the coach. Both men put their hands to their guns. 'I don't much like being told what to do by some stuck-up little English girl.'

'Please, don't take offence,' said Andrew. 'My sister is tired. We've been travelling for many weeks now.'

'Your sister, eh?' said Bill. 'That's what they all say.'

The younger man cackled, and made an offensive remark about the nature of Bella and Andrew's relationship.

Bella longed for her brother to say something, but he just sat back in silence, forcing her to speak again.

'We are brother and sister,' she said, 'and I resent the implication that we're not. Now please, if you don't abide by the rules, I'll be forced to speak to the driver.'

At that, Bill burst out laughing. 'He'll be dead two minutes later,' he said, his hand still fingering the trigger of his gun.

'And you'll be dead two minutes after

that.' A rifle appeared out of the long, black coat, and the man in the corner sat up and straightened his hat. He was in his mid-thirties, his piercing blue eyes rimmed with dark lashes. The effect against his tanned skin was startling. His cheekbones were finely carved, almost Slavic, and his mouth sensuous. He turned to look at Bill. 'Do as the young lady asks, and abide by the rules.'

Despite having the slow drawl characteristic of American inhabitants, and a tone that brought to mind a low growl, his voice was more cultured than Bill and Tom's.

Bill went for his gun, but in the confines of the coach, the man in black was quicker. In an instant he pushed the rifle against Bill's chest. Tom reached for his gun, and then thought better of it.

'Now you and I know something that the young lady and her brother don't know,' the man in black said, putting extra emphasis on the word *brother*. 'If you kill the driver of the mail coach, it is a federal offence,' he said, 'liable to get your name on posters all over the country, and a rope on a tree outside some small town. And you two look strictly small time to me.'

'Maybe we could just kill you,' said Tom, his voice wavering. 'You ain't nobody special.'

'Yeah, who the hell are you?' said Bill. 'I wanna know before I kill you.'

With the rifle still pressed against his chest, there did not seem to be much chance of that.

'Me?' The man in black smiled, showing even, white teeth. He opened his coat slightly, revealing the glint of a silver badge. 'I'm just a college boy.'

★   ★   ★

'Forgive me for not introducing myself sooner,' said the man in black. Tom and Bill had been deposited on the roadside and told to find another way home. The coach continued its journey with just three passengers. 'We had word there may be some trouble on this coach and I was asked to come along incognito. My name is Vance Eagleson. I'm a federal marshal.'

'I'm very pleased to meet you, Sir,' said Andrew, holding out his hand. 'I'm Andrew Tennyson and this is my sister, Miss Bella Tennyson.'

Bella inclined her head and smiled shyly. Though not big in the sense of the uncouth Bill, Vance Eagleson seemed to dominate the carriage.

'What brings you folks all the way from England?' asked Vance.

'Our aunt died last year and we've come out to claim her land,' said Andrew. 'It's in a town called Milton. In . . . ' he paused, and looked to Bella for confirmation.

'The Sierra Nevada,' said Bella.

'Milton's where I'm headed too,' said Vance, nodding. 'They've had some problems keeping their marshals lately, so I've been appointed by the government to the role.'

'Is it true they've been murdered?' asked Bella, wide-eyed.

'Yes, ma'am. I don't know how much you know about where you're going, but civilisation has been slow arriving in the west.'

'I have been warned it isn't a safe place for my sister,' said Andrew.

'You were told right, Mister Tennyson. Milton is still a dirt town at the moment. They haven't even got the railroad yet. As far as I know, it's got a couple of stores, a saloon and a . . . ' Vance paused, 'Well, some things aren't fit for a young lady's ears.'

'But there are vineyards there, aren't there?' said Bella.

'Yes, ma'am. Just outside the town limits, I believe. I hear they make some very fine wines. The workers used to be Chinese, which brought its own problems.'

'You don't like the Chinese?' said Bella.

'I like them fine, ma'am. I knew a lot of Chinese folk back in Chicago.

Unfortunately, as you heard old Bill there say, anyone whose skin isn't whiter than white is not particularly welcome around these parts. There's been a lot of animosity towards Chinese vineyard workers in the Sierra Nevada, because now white settlers are moving there, they want to keep the work for themselves.'

'Is it true your grandfather was a Cherokee?' asked Andrew, his eyes shining with excitement. During their long journey he had regaled Bella with stories of Indian ambushes, whilst assuring her such things seldom happened any more.

'My great grandfather, yes. I hope that doesn't make you sorry to be sharing this coach with me?'

'No, not at all,' said Bella. She wanted to tell him that he was a man she felt they could trust, and that nothing else mattered, only shyness prevented her. 'We're very grateful for your intervention with those men.'

'A word of warning, ma'am. It's not

always a good idea to challenge folks around here. Men get killed for a lot less.'

Bella looked at her brother, and once again wondered what sort of land he had brought her to.

A few hours later the coach finally arrived in Milton as the sun began to set. Vance Eagleson told them to wait whilst he found out if they could get a driver to take them out to their aunt's place. They waited by their trunks until he returned.

The town was much as he had told them. The wide road was a muddy track and, within minutes, the hem of Bella's travelling skirt was caked in dirt, despite the fact she had barely walked on it. There was a hardware store, which also appeared to sell a myriad of other items, and a telegraph office on one side of the street. Across from them was the saloon, and next door to that an establishment called Aunt Kitty's.

The only other buildings in the town were a blacksmiths, the marshal's office attached to the jail, a makeshift wooden church some two hundred yards out of town and, next to that, a small building that appeared to be the schoolhouse. If there were any homes in the vicinity, they could not be seen from where they were.

Piano music emanated from the saloon, along with the sound of men talking, but the streets were empty.

'I'm sorry, Bella,' said Andrew again, as they waited for the marshal to come back.

'Stop it!' she snapped.

'What?'

'Saying sorry. We're here now; we have to make the best of it.'

'You're still angry with me.'

'No, I'm not angry with you. But it's fair to say that if not for you, I could be at home, in our own country, instead of this god-forsaken place.'

Bella was intelligent enough to know deep down that she was being unfair to their new home. Quite apart from the fact she was first seeing it through a haze of exhaustion, homesickness was rendering her irrational.

'If only I were as perfect as you are, Bella,' Andrew said, his voice tinged with bitterness. 'It must be wonderful to always be right.'

'I'm not always right,' said Bella, her eyes too dry from exhaustion to shed tears. 'I . . . '

'Ma'am, sir.' It was Vance. Bella wondered how long he had been there. 'They tell me that your aunt's place is an hour's drive out of town. Perhaps it would be best if you stayed here tonight, and travelled up in the morning.'

'No, I want to go tonight,' said Bella. 'I mean, sorry, but I'd just like to end this journey.'

'I understand that, ma'am, but no one will take you up there in the dark. Besides, you've no idea what state the place is in. You'd be better seeing it in daytime, when you're less exhausted. The saloon has a couple of rooms spare. You could stay there and travel up in the morning.'

'I suppose we could stay at the saloon,' said Bella, her heart sinking.

'Do they play cards in there?' Andrew asked.

Bella's heart sank. That was all she needed.

'I guess so,' said Vance. 'But you folks look tired. Why don't you get some rest? I have to go report for duty now, but if there's anything you need, I'll be at the jailhouse.'

'Thank you for all your help, marshal.' Bella held out her hand, and he took it in his, holding it for just a bit longer than necessary.

In his strong handshake he seemed to tell her he understood everything. But how could he?

'Anytime. Like I said, call on me if you need anything.'

Bella said a quiet goodnight, before following her brother to the saloon.

2

Despite her misgivings about sleeping at the saloon, Bella had a good night's rest, no doubt due to her utter exhaustion.

The following morning, she dressed and knocked on her brother's door. He did not answer.

'Do you know if my brother is still in his room?' she asked the bartender when she went downstairs.

'Yes, ma'am. He had a late night. Said not to wake him too early.'

Bella sighed. 'I need to wake him,' she said. 'Where can I arrange for a driver to take us to my aunt's vineyard?'

'Go to the blacksmiths. He'll get one of his boys to take you and your luggage up there in a buckboard.'

'Thank you.'

Bella walked to the blacksmiths but there was no one around.

'Morning, ma'am.'

'Marshal, good morning.' Bella turned and smiled. At the moment Vance Eagleson was the only familiar face she knew, and a welcome addition to her morning at that. 'I'm trying to arrange a buckboard — whatever that is — to take us up to the vineyard, but I can't find anyone.'

'I think the blacksmith had to go and shoe some horses for one of the ranchers. I'll be happy to take you up to your place.'

'I don't want to put you to any trouble.'

'It's no trouble at all, ma'am. I'm going to introduce myself to a few folks in the area, and you're on my way. Where is Mister Tennyson this morning?'

'He's still sleeping.'

'Then why don't you leave him here, and he can get a ride up later?'

Bella was surprised by how attractive Vance's suggestion seemed. She had spent every day for three months with

17

her brother. It might do them both good to have a few hours' break.

★ ★ ★

Half an hour later, the luggage was loaded onto the marshal's buckboard, which turned out to be a four-wheeled wagon, pulled by a horse. The buckboard in question was a piece of wood at the front that acted as both a footrest and a barrier against a kicking horse.

Bella had left a message for her brother to join her.

Vance took her up into the hills, where the land became prettier. The sky overhead was sapphire blue. Ruby and emerald vineyards rested among a wheaten patchwork quilt. In the far distance she could see the snow-covered range.

'That's why it's called the Sierra Nevada,' Vance told her. 'It means 'snowy mountain range'.'

'It's beautiful.' Bella smiled. 'Though I must confess I was getting a little tired of scenery.'

'Yep, it gets you like that when you first see this land. It's beautiful, but it can be overwhelming.'

'But you were born here.'

'In Chicago, ma'am. Not out here, in this wilderness.' He paused for a moment. 'I noticed some tension between you and your brother yesterday. Is it anything you'd like to talk about?'

Bella thought about it for a short time. 'I don't want to burden you . . . '

'You won't be doing that. Maybe I can help?'

'No, you can't help, marshal. My brother . . . well, he has a problem.'

'Gambling?'

'It's that obvious?'

'He was playing cards into the early hours. One of the deputies saw him in the saloon.'

'He promised me . . . '

'I've seen a lot of men run out of their homes due to gambling debts. Is that why you had to leave England?'

Bella nodded. 'He owed money to the wrong people. We had no choice but to run away. Luckily we got the news about Aunt Bella's vineyard. I suppose we could have sold it, to pay off his debts, but it seemed better to try and make a new start.'

'Your mom and dad couldn't help?'

She shook her head. 'Mother died when I was ten and Andrew was fifteen. Father died two years ago. In a way it's a blessing. He never knew quite how bad Andrew's problem was, and for that I'm grateful.'

'Must have been hard for you, leaving it all. Did you leave behind a sweetheart? Back in England?'

Bella laughed. 'No. There was no one. What about you? Have you a sweetheart in Chicago?'

A few seconds later, Bella wished she had never asked.

'Yes, ma'am. I'm engaged to a fine lady called Gloria. As soon as I'm settled out here, and found us some-where to live, she's going to join me.'

'That's wonderful. Congratulations,' said Bella. Why her heart should sink as it did, she did not understand. It was natural that such a handsome man should have a woman in his life.

'Thank you, ma'am.'

They drove in silence for a while, and the empty land of the valley changed to vineyards, ranches and homesteads. Bella felt safe with him, and free from the tension that had been such a big part of her relationship with her brother for so many months.

'Aren't you afraid of being here?' asked Bella. 'After what's happened to the other marshals.'

'I can take care of myself, ma'am.'

'I'm sure they thought they could too.'

'From what I hear, one was a drunk and the other a cattle rustler. They don't always pick good men for this job. Just whoever's available. At least at a local level. The US Marshals Service is a little different.'

'So why were they killed?'

'It seems they outlived their usefulness.'

'I don't understand,' Bella turned slightly to look at him.

'There's a man in the area, name of Arthur Griffiths. A big landowner. People round here pretty much do as he says. And if they don't, or they try to double cross him in any way, they have a habit of turning up dead.'

'He kills them?'

'No, he's too clever for that. Or too scared to get his own hands dirty. He's got people to do it for him. Your brother should never have brought you here.'

'Yet you're bringing Gloria.'

'No offence, ma'am, but Gloria is an American girl, born and bred. She can skin a rabbit before it even knows it's been caught.' He turned and fixed his vivid eyes on Bella. 'You, you're like a delicate flower who needs sheltering from the storm.'

'That's a very romantic observation, marshal, but you obviously haven't met many English women. Appearances can be deceptive.'

'Then I look forward to seeing you prove me wrong. But not too wrong, you hear. Let me keep some ideals.'

As they finally turned into the approach to her late aunt's vineyard, she wondered why, with the resourceful Gloria to hand, he should care?

A big sign proclaimed that they had reached Bella's Vineyard. The months rolled away, as Bella saw for the first time the land she and her brother had come to claim. The vineyards themselves were overgrown, but she could still see the signs of cultivation and there appeared to have been some attempt at pruning the row near to the approach road. At the far end of the eastern vineyards was a river, which Bella assumed came down from the white-topped mountains that rose up behind the land.

At the top of the road, nearly a mile from where the approach began, stood a large white house, different to what Bella had expected. From what she had seen on their travels, she had envisaged a wooden shack, with just a couple of rooms. It was clear that this house had started out that way, and the original building could be seen at the centre. But someone had built onto it, adding a veranda and a top floor, with a gabled roof. One of the windows was broken, and the shuttering needed a lick of paint, but it showed every sign of being a solid homestead.

'It's very pretty, ma'am,' said Vance, pulling up the buggy.

'Yes, it is,' said Bella. 'I wasn't expecting . . . ' She smiled, ready to cry with relief.

The porch swing waved invitingly in the breeze, luring Bella with its relaxing sway. 'My aunt has been dead two years,' she said. 'I thought it would be falling down.'

'Put your hands in the air, and get down off the buggy!'

Bella and Vance spun around to see where the voice had come from. It seemed to be coming from somewhere within the vineyard. From a distance, Bella thought it was a man. As their assailant drew nearer, it became clear it was a woman in her fifties. She was dressed in a checked shirt, leather chaps, and wearing a Stetson set back on her head. Her black hair was cut short, like a man's. Bella had never seen anyone like her.

'Ma'am,' Vance started to say, only for the woman to shoot at the wheel of their buggy.

'Get off my land.'

'Your land?' said Bella. 'But . . . Aunt Bella? I thought you were dead.'

'Aunt Bella? I'm not Bella. Are you . . . ? Well, stone me.' The woman put the rifle down. 'It's okay, it's okay, I ain't gonna shoot you.'

Despite her assurances, both Bella and Vance stepped down from the buggy slowly.

'My name is Bella Tennyson. My aunt owned this land and left it . . . ' Bella stopped. She had promised Andrew she would not say anything.

'Yes, yes, I know,' said the woman. 'Well, I'll be darned. I never thought you'd come. I've been protecting this place for months from that varmint

Griffiths. Where are my manners?' The woman emerged from the vineyard, and held out her hand, but not before rubbing it on her shirt. 'My name is Maylene Tucker. My friends call me May. I was your aunt's . . . ' she paused momentarily, and her bright, brave eyes became sad, 'housekeeper and friend. And is this your brother? That's mighty odd. He looks part Indian to me.' It was said with curiosity rather than malice.

'No.' Bella smiled. 'This is Marshal Eagleson. My brother, Andrew, will be arriving later today.'

Vance held out his hand and was rewarded with a vigorous shake of May's. He clearly found the whole thing amusing.

'Mighty glad to meet you, marshal. I hope you ain't gonna go and die on us like them others.'

'I'll try my best not to, ma'am.'

'Well, that's what they all say, but it's a different story when they're complaining about the ride up to Boot Hill in the hearse.'

Bella looked at Vance, then turned away, her throat bubbling with laughter. Considering that two men had died, it was not funny, but May had a particular way of putting things.

'You say you've been keeping an eye on the place. Thank you,' she said to May once she had composed herself.

'There's no need to thank me. I did it for your aunt. You've her look about you, you know.' May paused again and that same sadness filled her eyes. 'Not that I've done much good keeping an eye on the place. Some kids came up here yesterday whilst I was out getting supplies and broke the top window. If I'd been here, I'd have given them a butt full of buckshot.'

'Do you live in the town?' asked Bella.

May paused for even longer. 'Yeah, I guess I do now.'

'Oh, of course, you used to live here, with Aunt Bella.'

'We kinda looked out for each other, you know. Neither of us having a

27

husband and all that.'

Bella sensed there were some things being left unspoken, but she did not want to pry.

'I'd ask you to stay but the trouble is, I don't know if I can afford to pay for a housekeeper.'

'I ain't got nowhere else to go,' said May candidly. 'And Bella would want me to take care of you.'

Bella immediately warmed to this doughty woman. 'I must admit I'd like some female company after three months on the road with my brother. Apart from the marshal, we don't have any friends here.'

'When you pick friends, you sure pick 'em well,' said May, looking the marshal up and down and winking at Bella.

'I'll leave you two ladies to get to know each other,' said Vance, after he had helped them carry the luggage into the house.

'Yes, thank you,' said Bella, turning to hold out her hand. The pressure of his hand on hers gave her an unexpected thrill. He showed none of the hesitant behaviour of the young men she had known in England. Yet his stillness continued to unnerve her. It was like he was holding something in and that it would become a raging torrent should he ever let it loose.

'I'll call on you in a few days, see how you're getting on,' he said.

'Please do. When we're settled, perhaps you could come up for dinner? We owe you that at least.'

'You don't owe me anything, ma'am, but I'll accept your offer anyway.' He tilted his hat, first to her, then to May Tucker.

Bella felt less apprehensive about being left at the house now that she had May by her side.

Inside was just as pretty as outside.

'You've kept it lovely, May,' she said, after May had given her a tour.

Downstairs there were three main rooms, a parlour, a dining room, and the kitchen, which also had a dining area, with a big, wooden table. Off the kitchen was a small washroom, complete with a tin bath. Upstairs were four bedrooms. May showed Bella into her aunt's old room.

'But don't you sleep in this room now?' said Bella, on seeing an old nightdress folded neatly at the foot of the bed and a pair of muddy boots at the far side.

'Well, just while I was keeping an eye on the place. I'll sleep in the back room from now on.'

'I can't put you out,' said Bella.

'Yes, you can. I gotta move out sometime. I can start by doing it one room at a time. We need to get that window fixed though. I don't mind the hole. It gets hot enough in summer. But come winter, you'll know about it. Come on, I'll show you outside.'

'The privy is there,' May pointed to a small hut further down the yard. 'We've got cellars underground. They're not as well stocked as they were, but there's a few bottles left down there. I'll find us a good wine to have with dinner. And here's the water pump. The water comes right in from the river,' May informed her, showing her the stand-pipe in the back yard. 'Me an' your aunt built the filtration system from a book we found in the city.'

'That's amazing,' said Bella.

'Yep, it's also why Griffiths wants to get his hands on this place. If he controls the water, he controls the town. Simple as that.'

'How?'

'The other farmers pay to graze their cattle. Your aunt never charged them much. Mostly in kind. You know, some potatoes, some beefsteak, hay for the horses, that kind of thing. If Griffiths got this place, he'd build a dam and make sure everyone paid through the nose for grazing rights.'

'But the water is free,' said Bella. 'It comes from the mountain. How can he control it?'

May laughed. 'Welcome to the United States of America, honey. The land of opportunity.'

* * *

It was the following day when Bella got her first glimpse of Arthur Griffiths. Her brother had failed to arrive from the town. Word came late in the day that he may travel up in the morning. When the morning came, and there was no sign of Andrew, Bella became apprehensive.

'You say he liked to gamble?' said May over breakfast. Bella had confided much in her over dinner the night before.

'Yes.'

'I'm sorry, honey. He ain't coming home till he's broke. Lots of men around here the same. Dig out gold all day from the mine, then go and gamble it away.'

'Then this is the worst place we could have come,' said Bella. She went out onto the porch. The day before, after meeting May, and finally reaching a place she could call home, she had felt happy. If she were honest, Vance

Eagleson had a little to do with that. She felt secure with him as a friend. As she looked out over the vineyard, she realised that the problem with running away from home was that you had to take yourself with you. Or, in her case, Andrew. His problems would be the same no matter where they were. From what she had seen of the saloon, it was as much a part of life in America as driving cattle and owning a six-gun.

Her heart lightened briefly when she saw some figures riding up the approach on horses. There were three, and the sunlight made them look like silhouettes, but she thought it might be Andrew with Vance Eagleson and maybe someone Andrew had befriended.

'Oh no,' Bella said quietly when they came into view.

'What is it, honey?' asked May, coming out onto the porch beside her.

'Those two men coming up the approach. They're the ones I told you about. From the coach. Bill and Tom. Who's that with them?'

'That's Arthur Griffiths. Now don't you let him bully you, honey. I'll be here to take care of you. Don't you worry none about Bill either.'

Arthur Griffiths was a surprise to Bella. She had imagined him to be overweight, with a beard. In short, another version of Bill and Tom. However, Griffiths was about fifty years old, but still handsome, his dark hair streaked with grey, giving him a distinguished air.

The three men finally reached the porch and dismounted.

'Ma'am,' said Mr Griffiths, raising his hat with an easy smile. He turned and scowled at Tom and Bill, who raised their own hats, smirking as they greeted her. 'My name is Arthur Griffiths. I came to welcome you to the neighbour-hood, though I must say, ma'am, I never expected to meet any one quite so young and beautiful.'

He put Bella in mind of the salesman who used to call at their door selling household goods. For the sake of good manners, she stepped down from the porch and held out her hand. Griffith's handshake, though strong enough, reminded her of a papier-mâché mask she had once made as a child. Cold, dry, and hollow.

'Mr Griffiths. I'm Bella Tennyson. I'm afraid my brother is not here at the moment. Perhaps you know . . . ' she turned to introduce May, who was scowling at Bill and Tom.

'They know me,' said May. 'Bill here is my brother.'

'Oh.' Bella felt the heat rising in her face. She had been less than complimentary when describing him to May.

'It's okay, honey,' said May. 'We ain't friends like you and your brother.'

'Actually, Miss Tennyson,' said Mr Griffiths, 'the reason I brought Bill and Tom here today is so they can apologise to you. They told me what happened on the stagecoach. I wanted you to know I will not tolerate that sort of behaviour in front of a lady.' Griffiths turned to each man and coughed slightly.

'I'm mighty sorry if I offended you, ma'am,' said Tom.

Bill and his sister were still locked in a scowling match.

'Bill! Do you have something to say to Miss Tennyson?'

'Sure. I'm sorry, ma'am.'

'I hope they're going to apologise to the marshal, too,' said Bella.

His pause lasted less than a moment, but it was enough to tell Bella all she needed to know about Arthur Griffiths.

'Of course,' he said, with a smile that failed to reach his eyes. 'I'll see they do that as soon as they next see him.'

3

Looks to me like you're gonna get your chance now,' said May, gesturing towards the approach.

Bella's heart lightened at the sight of Vance riding towards them. He had swapped the buggy for a black stallion, casting Mr Griffiths and the two men into insignificance with his proud bearing.

'Good morning,' he said, when he reached them. He raised his hat to Bella and May, then jumped down from the horse in one lithe movement.

'Good morning,' she said, her pretty face breaking into a genuine smile. 'Have you met Mr Griffiths?'

She knew that he understood the guarded tone of her voice, because his eyes darkened slightly, before he composed himself and held out his hand.

'Mr Griffiths, I've heard a lot about you.'

Bella felt her cheeks flame when Griffiths ignored the outstretched hand. As the hostess of this awkward gathering, she felt somehow responsible.

'I've heard a lot about you too, marshal,' said Griffiths. 'I gather my men here gave you a hard time yesterday. Bill. Tom. Do you have something to say to the marshal?'

'Boss, you're not really gonna make us . . . ' Bill got no further before Griffiths turned to face him head on. His eyes held a stark warning, but also something else. Conspiracy.

Bill hesitated. 'We're sorry we caused trouble.' He followed the empty apology by spitting on the ground.

'We're sorry,' said Tom, joining his older companion in another spitting contest. Bella felt her stomach turn, but she ignored them.

'I hope we can get along well together,' Griffiths was saying to Vance. 'I'm sure we both have the best interests of the people of Milton in mind.'

'I'm sure we have,' said Vance. His manner was polite, but cautious.

'Now if you'll excuse us.' Griffiths turned to Bella and raised his hat. 'I wanted to discuss some business with your brother, Miss Tennyson, but I guess that's going to have to wait for another day.'

'Anything you want to ask my brother, you can ask me,' said Bella.

Griffiths cast her a withering look, but his voice was all charm. 'There are some things ladies should not have to worry their pretty heads about. Maybe I'll call on your brother in the saloon later. I prefer to do business over a drink and a game of cards.'

Bella's face flushed again. Did everyone know about Andrew's problem?

'There ain't many secrets in Milton,' May muttered, as Griffiths, Bill and Tom rode away. She looked from Bella to Vance, smiling enigmatically, before going into the house.

'I'm glad you came,' Bella said to Vance. 'I don't think I like that man.'

'No, and he certainly doesn't like me,' said Vance.

'I'm sorry he was so rude to you.'

'I never expected anything else, coming here as a state-appointed marshal. I daresay Griffiths would have liked to put his own man in the job.'

'May has made some coffee,' said Bella. 'Would you like some? Have you eaten? There's plenty of breakfast left. Judging by all the pancakes, I think May's used to feeding an army.'

Vance smiled. 'I'd love some. Thank you, ma'am.'

'Please stop calling me ma'am. It makes me feel like an old woman. I think we can consider ourselves friends now, and my friends call me Bella.'

'Okay, Bella.' The way he said her name in his resonant tone sent a small flame of pleasure down her spine.

As Bella led him to the kitchen, she almost tripped over a box on the floor. She picked it up and put it on the table. It had air holes in the top and a wire mesh door at one end.

'Is that a rabbit?' asked Vance.

'Yes, I'm going to cook it for supper,' said Bella.

'I think they're supposed to be dead.'

'Well, obviously. But I thought I'd eat breakfast before I started cutting its throat.'

The rabbit looked up at them both with big, brown eyes.

'It looks to me like it knows it's been caught,' said Vance.

'I did intend skinning it without its knowledge, but it took me an hour to catch it. We were both a little exhausted by the time I'd put him in the trap.'

Vance laughed. 'So you're really gonna kill it?'

Bella blushed. 'Of course. May says I need to toughen up after I refused to choose the cow for our steak last night. Call me squeamish, but it's hard to eat something I've looked in the eye. I'm used to a butcher sorting all that out for me.'

'This rabbit has looked you in the eye.'

41

'I'm not going to let that bother me any more. If you don't believe me, come by for dinner and we'll share our rabbit stew with you.'

May and Vance exchanged knowing glances and a conspiratorial smile.

'I think I know who's won this battle,' said Vance, throwing his hat onto the table and sitting down.

'Do you want bacon and eggs? I can rustle up some grits?' May asked, bustling around Vance five minutes later as he sat with Bella in the kitchen. They sipped on coffee, and made small talk.

'No thank you, Miss Tucker. These pancakes will do me just fine.'

'May, come and sit down with us,' said Bella. 'You've done enough this morning already.'

Bella felt guilty that May had fallen so quickly back into the role of housekeeper. Bella was also very aware that the food they ate had been supplied by May. She would have to check her own money, which was stowed safely away in the bottom of her trunk out of Andrew's reach, and pay May back.

'I've got cleaning to do. Besides, you two young 'uns don't want an old woman hanging around you.'

'May, you don't have to . . . ' May was gone before Bella had even finished her sentence.

'I wish I could pay her a wage,' she said to Vance.

'I gather she's okay for money,' said Vance. 'Her father was one of the early prospectors. Did better out of the mines than most men who came later. Pretty shrewd with his money too, I hear.'

'You wouldn't think it looking at Bill Tucker.' Bella wondered why May worked as a housekeeper when she had money. 'Oh, did you know? The older man we met on the coach is her brother.'

'No, I didn't know that. Well, that makes me worry a little less. He'll probably leave you alone now.'

'You don't have to worry about me,'

said Bella, secretly thinking that there was so much obvious bad blood between May and Bill there was no guarantee of any security in the connection.

'You're not in England any more, Bella. Everyone out here lives in relative isolation, so help is often a long time coming. It mightn't hurt if you could get a guy up here to keep watch.'

'Andrew will come soon,' said Bella, sounding doubtful even to herself.

'Your brother is not the sort of man I'm thinking of,' said Vance. 'I mean someone who's handy with a gun, and who can maybe help you out around the place.'

'I've been talking to May about getting the vineyard up and running again,' said Bella. 'She says it might take a couple of years before we can start to grow decent crops, but she knows some of the Chinese men who used to work here, before Griffiths and his men chased them off. She's going to approach them and ask if they'll be willing to work in return for some of the profits.'

'That's not a bad idea. How can she be sure they'll come back?'

'She thinks things have changed. The other landowners are starting to resent Griffiths, whereas before they all fell into place behind him. Apart from Aunt Bella. She knew all along he was no good.'

'You know he wants to buy this place off your brother?'

Bella was silent for a moment. 'I had a feeling that's why he wanted to talk to Andrew. He's wasting his time, though. The vineyard isn't for sale.'

'Your brother might have other ideas.'

'I don't care. It's not for sale. I gave up everything to come here. I'm not about to turn around and go back again.'

Vance looked at her for such a long time that she began to feel self-conscious. She knew her hair was not as neat as it could have been and she was wearing an old, blue gingham dress of her aunt's, having been too exhausted to unpack clean clothes the night before.

'You were right about English women, weren't you?'

Bella smiled. 'I told you not to underestimate us.'

'I don't, Bella. But you shouldn't underestimate Griffiths and what he's willing to do to win this place. Men like him don't have the same sense of fair play that most decent folk do.'

Bella shivered, feeling for a moment as if the sun had gone in. 'Let's talk about happier things,' she said. 'When will we meet Gloria? I was thinking last night if she needed somewhere to stay, I mean, if she came to visit you, she'd be very welcome here.'

Bella had thought no such thing, and could not comprehend why she'd suddenly blurted out the offer.

Vance stayed for a little while longer, and then started back for the town.

'You did good catching that rabbit,' he said, when he was sitting on his horse ready to go. 'But it was a bad idea not to kill it immediately. They sense weakness. Whatever you do, don't let him talk you into giving him a name between now and supper time.' He winked at her and rode away.

She turned and went back into the house, thinking that it was time she unpacked her clothes. But first she went to the rabbit in the kitchen. She gently lifted him out of the box and held him close, feeling his velvety soft fur against her cheek.

'Because you fought so valiantly, I'm going to call you Hector.'

★ ★ ★

'I'm just going out to talk to Shen,' said May, coming downstairs wearing her riding jacket as Bella was on her way upstairs to unpack. 'I hear he's working at one of the gold mines.'

'Will Shen want to come here if there's gold to be found in the mines?' asked Bella.

47

'Ain't much gold left, honey. Most of the prospectors have taken it. It's just penny ante stuff nowadays. Enough to buy a man a meal a day and a room above the saloon.'

'But it's still more than I can pay,' said Bella.

'Viticulture is in Shen's blood,' said May. 'I think he'll come back just for the pleasure of doing something he's good at.'

'Well if you think he will, then ask. Make sure the terms are fair, May. I don't agree with slavery. Which reminds me, before you go, let me give you some money for the food and a couple of week's wages. I can't pay you beyond that but perhaps something will turn up by then. I could find work in the town.'

'There's only one type of work for a young lady in Milton and even if I couldn't stop you, I reckon that handsome marshal would have something to say about it. I don't want anything. Your aunt took care of me when . . . '

Ignoring May's protestations, Bella skipped up the stairs to her bedroom, taking the key to her trunk from the chain she had around her neck. Five minutes later, she sat on the floor, frantically searching the trunk, throwing clothes all over the room, shaking out undergarments and dresses.

'It's here, I know it's here,' she said, fighting back the tears that threatened to flow.

'What, honey? What's wrong?' said May from the door.

'My money. It was in my trunk. I last had it in . . . ' Bella stopped and sat back on her heels, remembering the chain of events. 'The night before last in the saloon. I must have left the key in the lock after I took out my night-clothes. I only went downstairs to get some water, and when I came back, Andrew was in my room. He's taken it, May. The only money I had — we had — in the world and he's taken it.' Bella burst into tears.

May knelt next to her and put her

49

arm around her shoulder. 'We'll work it out, honey, don't you worry. I can loan you some.'

'No,' said Bella. 'I can't do that. I barely know you, and already I owe you more than I can possibly repay.'

'Your aunt was my friend. She was like a sister to me. Which kinda makes you family.'

'May, that's really sweet, but . . . '

'Thirty years ago,' said May, emphatically ignoring Bella, 'my daddy turned me out of the house. I had nothing then and nowhere to go. It was your aunt who took me in. I only came into money when my father died, and then it was because my mama insisted he left me something for all those years I used to help him work the mine. So I owe your family much more than you could ever owe me.'

'I will pay you back,' said Bella some time later. She had spent half an hour with her back against the wardrobe, thinking about what to do, whilst May set about tidying away the discarded clothes. She saw no other way than to accept May's charity. She couldn't go back to England because she didn't have the money, but she could at least try to go forward.

'We'll get the vineyard working together, you and I, and we'll share the money we make.'

'If that's what you insist, then that's the way we'll do it. Darn it,' said May, her bright eyes shining with unshed tears, 'you're so much like your aunt. You've got that same determined little chin. She never let anyone or anything beat her.'

'I'm sure that's because she had you as a friend,' said Bella.

* * *

Andrew finally arrived later that evening, smelling of alcohol and swaying on his feet. Bella flew at him as he walked through the door.

'You stole my money, Andrew.'

'Bella, dearest, listen to me. I had a

winning hand. I could have . . . '

'Could have? Could have? But you didn't, did you? You've lost it all and now I have to rely on the charity of a woman I only met yesterday.' Bella hated how shrewish she sounded. For a long time she had felt more like Andrew's mother than his younger sister.

'God forbid that you should have to ask anyone for anything,' said Andrew, his voice rising, becoming hollow and ugly as it did. 'The perfectly wonderful Bella, who never does anything wrong.'

'Oh, I do things wrong,' said Bella. 'I was wrong to ever believe that I could change you by coming here.'

'Good lord, Bella, you're not my wife. Now stop nagging me and get me some food. I'm starving.'

'Don't speak to your sister like that, young man.'

'Who are you and what in damnation has it got to do with you?' asked Andrew, his eyes widening at the sight of the woman dressed in men's clothes standing in the kitchen doorway.

'This is May Tucker,' said Bella. 'She's Aunt Bella's friend and at the moment she's taking care of us, despite the fact we are not her problem. So I suggest you treat her with a little more respect.'

Andrew paused near the foot of the stairs, sizing May Tucker up. His high-pitched tones became soft and contrite, and Bella knew by his eyes that he was already working out how he could bring May onto his side.

'Bella, dearest, I'm sorry, I'm very tired. Miss Tucker, please accept my apologies for my rudeness.' He tipped his hat to her. 'Any friend of our aunt's is a friend of ours, and I'm very pleased to make your acquaintance.'

'Just don't let me hear you talk to Miss Bella like that again.'

'No, of course I won't. It's been a long trip, as I'm sure Bella will have told you. Unfortunately I managed to leave my manners somewhere along the way, for which I apologise. Now if you ladies will point me in the direction of a bedroom, I'll keep out of your way until I've regained them.'

'He soon changed his mood,' said May, once Andrew was upstairs and fast asleep.

The two women sat on the porch together, as fireflies danced around them. May had found a bottle of wine in the cellar, a deep red that tasted to Bella of raspberries and the earthy flavour of fresh vegetables. Along with the gentle sway of the porch swing, it calmed her nerves.

One of her family had to be strong, and even though Bella sometimes felt her back would break under the strain, she was determined to be the one.

'That's Andrew's way, I'm afraid,' said Bella. 'My father said that my mother indulged him too much when he was younger, and he'd throw these awful tantrums one moment, then when he realised he was in the wrong, he'd suddenly become contrite and boyish. My mother fell for it every time.

As have many of the women he's managed to persuade to give him money.'

'And you?'

'Not any more,' said Bella.

She thought of Vance Eagleson. How self-assured and calm he was. That, to her, was how a man should behave. With courage and dignity. If only her brother Andrew could develop some of the maturity her father used to promise he would achieve one day.

'Anyway,' said Bella, taking another fortifying sip of wine, 'did you manage to speak to Shen?'

'Yes, and he's agreed to our terms. I offered him and his men the bunkhouse. They can eat with us in the kitchen, if you've no objections.'

'None at all. It will be nice to know that your pile of pancakes won't be wasted in future. How many workers will we have?'

'About ten to start with. There's Shen, his two sons, a few brothers or brothers-in-law. Then there's me, you and your brother.'

'I think it will just be me and you,' said Bella sadly.

'Miss Bella, you're a kind, proud girl, but don't you think you should let your brother stand on his own two feet? One day, you'll meet a man you want to marry and your brother will have to sort out his own problems.'

'He's family, May. I can't leave him to his own devices. But I will be more careful in future. There's a bank in Milton, yes?'

'That's right.'

'We'll put all the money we earn in there. We won't keep anything in the house, and Andrew will just get an allowance. How he spends it is up to him. He'll just have food and a roof over his head. But I can't turn him out. You should understand that, better than anyone.'

May reached over and patted Bella's shoulder. 'Okay, we'll do it your way, but I ain't gonna tread on eggshells around him.'

Bella turned her head to May and smiled. 'I'm glad to hear it. It will do him good to realise he's not the apple of everyone's eye.'

'And what about that good-looking marshal? Is he going to be the apple of your eye?'

'I've told you, May, he's spoken for.'

'His fiancée's a long way away, and you're here. Last night he said he wouldn't see you for a few days, yet this morning he turns up again.'

'I think he feels responsible for us,' said Bella. 'Because of what happened on the coach.'

'You're a very smart young woman, honey, but I don't think you've much experience of men. I've seen the way he looks at you.'

'Now stop it,' said Bella, smiling sadly. 'If I dare to hope, I'll just get my heart broken.'

'So you have thought about him?'

'How could I not?' said Bella. 'There's something about him. A presence I've never seen in a man before. Whatever happens, I don't think I'll ever forget how he stood up to Tom and Bill on the coach. He was absolutely fearless. He was the same with Mr Griffiths today.'

She put her glass down on the floor with a loud thump. 'Oh, look at me, half a glass of wine and I'm talking like a silly schoolgirl.'

'That ain't the wine talking,' said May.

4

The days that followed kept Bella too busy to worry about Andrew. He came and went as he pleased — she did not ask where he got the money from — whilst other landowners called to welcome them to Milton.

Many promises were made about continuing to allow the water to flow and the cattle to graze. Landowners involved in the same business as Bella advised her on how to get her crops to bear fruit as quickly as possible.

'We all help each other out here,' said one landowner, Ike Peterson. He had arrived at the vineyard one morning with his wife, Henrietta. They sat around the table on the porch, drinking lemonade. 'We'd like to start by inviting you to our daughter's engagement party next Sunday.'

'Yes, do come,' said Henrietta. She

was a motherly woman, who Bella guessed had once been pretty, before blooming a little too well under the California sun. 'We're always short of young people at these affairs. The new marshal is coming. He's already caused quite a few hearts to flutter in the town.'

'He seems like a good man,' said Ike. 'He's already fired two deputies who were on Griffiths' payroll. Milton has a chance to thrive with a man like that in charge of law enforcement.'

Henrietta was more interested in the party than local politics. 'There'll be dancing, and food, and my husband has hired a band from Nevada city, haven't you, Ike?'

'You had her at 'the new marshal is coming',' May murmured at Bella's shoulder, as she put a plate of cookies on to the table. Bella hoped she was the only one to hear it.

'Your brother will also come, we hope,' said Henrietta. 'Such a hand-some young man. Between him and the marshal, the young ladies of Milton are spoiled for choice. Your brother is very polite. I met him in the town only the other day. I love the way he speaks. Like a real English lord.'

'We'd be delighted to attend,' said Bella. 'If my brother can't come, I'm sure May will be happy to take his place.'

There was an awkward silence. 'Yes, certainly,' said Ike. 'Certainly. You'll be very welcome Miss Tucker.'

'I doubt it,' said May, without a trace of malice in her voice. 'But I'm darned if I'm letting Bella travel back alone at night.'

When the Petersons had left, Bella found May in the kitchen. 'The Petersons weren't very warm towards you. Have you had a falling out with them at some point?'

May stopped washing the dishes and turned to face Bella. 'Honey, there's things you don't know about me. Things I've been afraid to tell you, in case it turns you against me. But I should have known it would become obvious, by the way people are with me.'

'Why are they like that, May?'

'I told you the other day that your aunt and me looked after each other because we didn't have husbands. The truth is, neither of us wanted a husband. Because . . . well . . . we had each other. Do you understand what I mean?' May paused to allow the significance to sink in. 'I didn't wanna tell you, you being such a nice young lady and all that. I'll understand if you'd rather I up and left.'

'Oh May, was that all?' Bella walked across the kitchen and took May's hand. 'I think I guessed on some level the day I arrived. It was the way you talked about Aunt Bella. And your boots being at the side of her bed.' Bella smiled and blushed a little. 'They seemed as if they'd been there all along. I knew there was a reason she left England all those years ago. The family secret, whispers at get-togethers, that sort of thing. Father always knew, I think, but he loved his sister, and always spoke of her with affection. I don't pretend to understand such things, but it seems to me that if you're lucky enough in this cold, hard world to find someone to love, and who loves you in return, then no one has the right to judge you or say you're wrong.'

'Honey, you truly are your aunt's niece. She'd have been so proud of you.' May's eyes filled with tears as she put her arms around Bella and hugged her roughly. 'Darn it, I'm proud of you, too.'

Over a cup of coffee at the kitchen table, May told Bella everything. About the dreadful time she tried to explain her feelings for Bella's aunt to her parents. That was when May's father turned her out. Her mother had tried to intervene on her behalf, but to no avail. May had to meet her mother in secret, but those were rare and precious occasions.

'It was the worst kept secret in Milton,' said May. 'Still is. I guess people just don't know how to take me. Oh, they're civil enough. I am a woman after all, so they think they have to be. Your aunt was okay, because she dressed like a lady all the time, so at least they could pretend she fitted in. I'm still not one of them. My brother . . . well, you met him. We never did like each other before I came here to live. I don't have to tell you his feelings on the matter. Since my mama died, and then your Aunt Bella, I've got no family to speak of.'

'Yes you have,' said Bella. 'If you were Aunt Bella's . . . ' she paused, 'intended, that makes you my aunty, too. I think. Goodness, it's complicated, isn't it?'

The two women looked at each other and burst out laughing.

★　★　★

Bella wanted to look her best for Amelia Peterson's engagement party. She told herself it was because she was making her debut in Milton society, and that it had nothing to do with the fact Vance would be there.

'What do the women wear to parties around here, May?' she asked. They were in her bedroom, and Bella was once again throwing dresses all over the floor. This time it was in frustration at finding nothing she felt was suitable. She had pretty dresses, but each time she held one up against herself in front of the mirror, she ended up imagining how Vance might see her, and was left feeling inadequate.

'You're asking me that?' May raised an eyebrow and gestured to her faded shirt and leather chaps.

'What have you seen them wearing?'

'Your aunt bought a really pretty dress just before she died. She was going to wear it to the Cattleman's Ball, but then she got sick. It's a pretty little garment. White lace, with ruffle type things here . . . ' May pointed to her shoulders, then shrugged. 'You'll find it in her wardrobe.'

Bella searched and found the dress

May described right at the back, still wrapped in tissue paper.

'We'll have to take it up a little,' Bella said to May as she looked at the dress. Her aunt had been a little bit taller than her. That didn't matter on day dresses, which were cut to midi-length, but the ball gown hung past Bella's feet. 'And I think the ruffles can go. It feels too fussy.'

By the time they had finished several hours later, the excess ruffles had been removed, leaving the dress with a clean-cut sweetheart neckline and a wide blue sash around the waist.

They were sitting at the kitchen table eating a hearty dinner of steak and fried potatoes when Andrew eventually arrived back from Milton.

'Bella, I've found a way to get out of this place,' he said, sitting down at the table. 'Arthur Griffiths has offered us a fair price for the vineyard. We can go back to England, pay off my debts and have enough to live on.'

'We're not selling the vineyard,

Andrew,' said Bella, putting down her knife and fork.

'Bella, dearest, at least think about it.'

'How much money do you owe?' she asked. Andrew looked at her and May sheepishly.

'Not much. I can soon pay it off. With your help.'

'I don't have any money. You took it all, remember.'

'Do we have to discuss this in front of the hired help?' asked Andrew, his voice rising to its familiar petulant tone.

'May isn't the hired help. She's family.'

'There are some things you don't know about her, Bella,' he said, glowering at May.

May stared him down, until he was forced to shift his gaze from her to the tablecloth.

'I know everything there is to know,' said Bella firmly. 'I know she's generous enough to keep us in food for a while.'

'Which is exactly what I'm talking about. If we sell the vineyard you can pay her back what you owe her, and then we can . . . '

'Andrew, I'm not going back. May and I have a plan to make the vineyard work. We won't be rich, but we'll be able to make a decent living. Of course, we'll need your help.'

'Me? You want me to work in the vineyard?' Andrew snorted.

'We have some Chinese workers starting tomorrow but, yes, we'll need help.' Bella knew it was futile to even ask, but she wanted to give Andrew a chance to show his mettle.

'I'm a gentleman,' said Andrew. 'Just as my father was a gentleman. You don't honestly expect me to get my hands dirty?'

'We've got to earn a living, Andrew. May and I can only do so much.'

Andrew stood up. 'You do what you want, but I'm not going to help you in this ridiculous undertaking.'

'Where are you going?' asked Bella.

'Back to Milton. I'm going to take a room there.'

'You don't have any money.'

'I'll do what I've been having to do all week. I'll borrow some until I win it back by my own skill at cards. At least I'm not relying on charity.'

Bella winced as Andrew slammed the front door behind him. 'Oh, May,' she said, pushing away her plate and putting her head in her hands. 'What am I to do with him?'

'You're to let him learn that in this country people don't get what they want just through birthright or winning it in a game of chance. They have to work for it.'

'I'd love him to be able to live the life of a gentleman,' said Bella, 'but it just isn't realistic. Not any more.'

'You're right. I don't like Griffiths very much, but the man hasn't been afraid to get his hands dirty.'

'Except when it comes to killing marshals,' said Bella, shivering.

'Well, maybe you're right on that score, too. He was respected as a young man. Not much liked, I'll grant you, he's always been too oily for that. It's only been in recent years he's started acting like he's some kind of god around the place.'

'What changed him do you think?'

'This country. It either makes or breaks a man. Sometimes it makes them then breaks them, when they realise they'll never be as big as those mountains over in the distance.'

'A man on the train said that men go mad out here. I suppose it doesn't really help if they were not that stable to begin with.' Bella was thinking of her brother as she spoke.

'No, honey, probably not.'

* * *

Over the days that followed, she tried not to worry about Andrew. There was a lot to do in the vineyard, and she had to attend the engagement party, despite the fact that she was not in the mood to socialise.

Shen, a refined old gentleman who

70

put Bella in mind of one of the three magi, arrived with his family and began to teach her all she needed to know about viticulture.

'We are over fifteen hundred feet above sea level,' he told her. 'That is perfect for wine-making, which is why there are so many vineyards in the Sierra Nevada. Our main enemies are phylloxera, an insect that feeds on the roots. And fire. Especially in this hot, dry weather. The plants become brittle, and can quickly go up in flames.'

Bella nodded, but understood very little of what he said.

'Do not worry, Miss Bella. You will soon learn. You are starting with all the tools you need. It costs a lot of money to develop a vineyard and can take up to four years before the grapes are ready to be harvested for wine. Your aunt has left everything you need, including the cellars and the ready-made vineyards. All these vines need now is love and attention.'

'How did you learn all this?' asked

Bella. 'What I mean is, I usually associate wine growing with the French.'

'It is the main profession of my family for many centuries. My father owned a vineyard when we first came here from China. But things are hard for us now. The Chinese Exclusion Act has prevented more of us from entering California and those of us who already live here cannot leave. I have not seen my wife for ten years, because I dare not leave, and she cannot come here.'

'I'm so sorry,' said Bella. 'I hope you are happy with May's offer. I don't want to be another person who treats you like a second class citizen.'

'You at least allow us to share the profits. Few Europeans will even allow that. The vineyards are my life. I enjoyed working for your aunt and I will enjoy working for you.'

Bella held out her hand and shook his. 'The feeling is mutual. Thank you.'

It was gruelling work, involving miles of walking and backbreaking pruning of the overgrown vines, but in many ways it helped her. She was too exhausted at the end of each day to think much about anything. One thing she did notice, however, was that Vance Eagleson had not been to visit since that second day. She knew he was busy with his new post, and that she could not expect his undivided attention. Still, she missed his calming presence in her life.

It was on the morning of the engagement party that he visited again. As he approached the vines where she was working, his face was grim.

'What is it? What's happened?' she said, shielding her eyes from the bright sunlight. 'Is it Andrew?'

'Yes,' said Vance, getting down from his horse. 'He's still alive, don't worry about that. I'm sorry, Bella, but I had to arrest him last night. He got into a brawl in the saloon. They say he was cheating at cards. I locked him up for his safety. I need you to vouch for him, and promise me that he'll stay here for a while. If he goes into town he's gonna get shot.'

Bella sighed. What else could she do?

'Yes, yes, of course. I'll come down and get him.'

Bella saddled up a horse for herself and one for Andrew. She had found some tan-coloured culottes of her aunt's, finding it much easier to sit astride the horse than riding side-saddle. It was how she had seen most of the young ladies of Milton ride, and gave her a sense of freedom she had never known.

'I'm sorry for the trouble Andrew has caused,' she said, as she and Vance rode towards Milton.

'He's lucky he's not dead, Bella. Men around here don't like cheats.'

'I'm sure he didn't cheat,' she said, hotly. 'Andrew is many things, but he's honest.'

'Is that why he stole the last of your money?'

'How did you know about that?' Bella's face burned crimson.

'He told me all about it while he was drunk last night. He's sorry, but I think that's more for being found out than actually taking it.'

'Anyway, that's different,' said Bella. 'I mean, stealing from family is not the same as cheating at cards, is it?'

'Maybe that's something for you to decide.' Vance fixed her with his intense gaze. 'Your brother has a sickness, Bella. One that few men can overcome, especially out here, where there's not much else to do.'

Bella looked up towards Vance, sitting high and proud in the saddle. She hated that he had such a low opinion of her brother, feeling that it reflected on her. She also hated that their easy friendship had become strained by Andrew's arrest.

'I'm sorry if this has caused you any problems,' she said again.

'I'm just doing my job,' he said. His voice softened. 'And sometimes I have to do things I'd rather not do. I'm only sorry that you're having to deal with this alone.'

'I'm not alone. I've got May. She's

been wonderful.'

'Miss Tucker is a very capable woman. Kind of scary too. But I feel a little happier knowing she's with you.'

'She thinks you're wonderful,' said Bella. 'So I don't think you have much to be afraid of. May chooses her friends well, I think.'

Vance brought his horse nearer and put his hand over Bella's. They were both wearing gloves, yet the very pressure of his hand sent a white-hot flame searing through her.

'I am your friend, Bella. I want you to remember that. No matter what might happen with your brother. No matter how many times I might have to arrest him. You might forget that, when you're angry with me, but it won't change the fact that whatever happens, I am your friend.'

'Why would I be angry with you?'

'Because it'll be easier than being angry with him. I just want you to know that I understand where your loyalties lie.'

'I'm sure it won't happen again, Vance. Andrew is just lost in a strange land, that's all. We all are. Me, you, Andrew, Shen, even May, who was born here. We're all outsiders in Milton.'

'That's true, but some of us care less than others.'

'Do you really not care, Vance? Or do you just pretend to survive the silent insults of men like Bill and Tom?'

'There's a saying. Those that matter don't mind and those that mind don't matter. I'm not gonna lose sleep over Griffiths. Besides, I'm not an outsider.' The corners of his mouth turned up, and he had a wry look in his eyes. 'My paternal ancestors were here long before the Europeans came. This is our land, and no amount of posturing by Griffiths or men like him is ever going to alter that.'

'Have you come to claim it back?' asked Bella with an impish grin.

Vance laughed. 'No. Well, not all of it. Just a little corner for myself.'

'I wish I could be more like you,' said

Bella. 'You're so certain of your place in this world.'

'Not always,' he said quietly. 'Do you think I'd be invited to the Peterson's party if I were full Cherokee? Or if it had been my father rather than my great-grandfather? I'm only in this job because I've got enough European in me to be palatable to the good citizens of Milton.'

'I'm sure that's not true,' said Bella.

'I'm pretty sure it is. My great-grandfather had a much tougher time of it than I do — his European wife was disowned by her family when she married him — but the bigotry is still there, under the surface.'

Bella did not know how to answer that. She was tempted to apologise for every white man alive. Sadly, she realised that anything she said would sound trite, or perhaps even patronising, and Vance Eagleson was not a man who would appreciate being spoken to in such a way. She did not want to add to the insults he endured.

'Your great-grandmother must have loved your great-grandfather very much,' she said. 'To be willing to give up so much for him.'

'Yes, I believe she did at first. But then she began to miss her family and the trappings of their riches. She blamed him for taking her away. She left him when my grandfather was a boy of ten, and returned to her people. They did all they could then to make sure my grandfather was brought up in European ways.'

'I'm sorry. I didn't realise.'

Bella had somehow forged a romantic idea of Vance's great-grandparents riding off into the sunset together to live happily ever after on a reservation. It made her sad to think that the love affair did not survive, after both must have made such a sacrifice to be together.

'But she kept his name, didn't she?' Ever the idealist, Bella wanted to believe that his great-grandmother continued to love the man she almost gave up everything for.

Vance shook his head. 'That was my father's doing. He didn't even know about his grandfather until he was a young man. He decided that we should be proud of our heritage. It was a brave thing to do, especially in this country. Luckily he had the money to cushion him against disapproval.'

'He sounds like a remarkable man.'

'He is. I respect him more than any other man alive.' He held up his head proudly, and Bella fancied she could see his father's determination in Vance's profile.

'Will he be coming to see you? I'd like to meet him.'

Vance's expression altered. 'No, he isn't too happy about my choice of career. He wanted me to go into the family business.'

'Which is?'

'Construction. My family built quite a lot of Chicago. I was meant to go to college and study architecture. I did for a while. Then I became interested in the law, and joined the United States

Marshals Service. The rest, as they say, is history. So was my relationship with my father for a while. He's mellowed of late, probably because of my engagement to Gloria, but he still expects me to go back to the family business one day.'

'How did you meet? You and Gloria, I mean.'

'We grew up together. Her father is my father's business partner. Since we were ten years old, the families had us set to marry. When she was eighteen she eloped with someone else, but he died a few years later.'

'You obviously love her very much.'

'You mean to forgive her for running off with another man? We weren't together then, despite what the families hoped. It was only last year when I went home for a visit that we started going steady.'

Bella could not help notice that he had not responded to her statement about loving Gloria. Or, she thought, maybe it was her own wishful thinking.

They rode in silence for a while, and then both started speaking at the same time.

'Is Gloria . . . ?' 'How are you settling . . . ?'

'Sorry, you first,' said Bella.

'No, ladies first.'

'I just wondered if she would be coming to join you soon.'

'As a matter of fact, I wrote to her just yesterday and suggested it. It's not as uncivilised here as I thought it might be. I reckon I could build us a nice house somewhere near the town.'

'Wonderful,' said Bella, feeling it was anything but. 'It's a pity she couldn't be with you tonight, for Amelia Peterson's engagement party.'

'Will you dance with me instead?'

Bella very nearly made a comment about being a consolation prize but swallowed it back. 'Yes, of course. It will save me from being a wallflower.'

'I don't think that'll happen.'

Andrew was in a contrite mood when Bella collected him from the jailhouse. He looked dirty and unshaven, not quite the gentleman he thought himself to be.

'I'm sorry for my behaviour last night, marshal,' he said, holding out his hand to Vance.

'Forget it,' said Vance. 'I just hope I don't have to offer you the hospitality of the jail in the future, Mister Tennyson. Will you be at the Peterson's place tonight?'

Bella hoped Andrew would not want to go. He was so unstable of late, she feared what might happen.

'Of course. Mrs Peterson asked me when I met her in town. I couldn't possibly let my sister go out amongst the wolves of Milton alone. Besides, Mister Griffiths is going to be there, isn't he? I met him yesterday. He's a good man, with a lot of ideas for rejuvenating Milton. I've got some business I want to discuss with him.'

Bella and Vance exchanged concerned glances. She shuddered when Andrew added, 'Mister Griffiths is rather taken with you, Bella.'

5

The Petersons had spared no expense in making their daughter's engagement a special occasion. When Bella and Andrew arrived in the buggy, they passed by trees filled with fairy lights. In the meadow behind the Peterson's sprawling one-storey house, there was a marquee, and outside a stage had been built, and a dance floor laid on one of the few flat pieces of ground in that part of the foothills.

Stirring banjo music flowed through the air, along with the thump of boots on the wooden floor, and a few cries of 'yeeha'.

Bella, wearing her aunt's white lace gown, had made a special effort with her hair, pinning it loosely at the sides. The rest hung down her back, shiny and golden.

'This is more like it,' said Andrew,

admiring the Peterson's home. 'I was beginning to think we'd moved to live among savages.'

'I'm sure you would get that impression if all your time is spent in the saloon.' The words were out before Bella could stop herself.

'Actually, dearest,' said Andrew, pulling the buggy into the corral set aside for visitor's vehicles, 'I wanted to talk to you about something. I know you're a kind-hearted girl who makes friends easily, but people are talking.'

'Talking?'

'First of all about the marshal. He seems to have made a pet of you, and well, he's . . . '

'Don't even say it, Andrew.' Bella's temper began to flare.

'Now, of course, it doesn't matter if you're just friends with someone. I'm not bigoted, you know that dearest, but, well, I wouldn't want a man like that to marry my sister.'

'Then you have no need to worry,' said Bella, in strained tones. 'Vance is already engaged to someone else.' The words sent tiny arrows shooting through her heart.

'He is? Well, I'm very happy for him. He is a good man, despite his pedigree, and I know you would never behave in a way that was immoral.'

Bella waited, sensing Andrew had something else to say.

'But that's not all, dearest. They say you've taken on a Chinese man to help on the vineyard. You know the Chinese are very unpopular here. The problem is so serious, they've had to bring in a law to get rid of them.'

'Everyone whose skin is not whiter than white is unpopular here,' said Bella. 'Shen is a good, hard-working man. But it should comfort you to know he's at least sixty years old and already married, so you've no worries on that score.'

'Now, don't be facetious, dearest.'

'I suppose May is going to be next on your list.'

'She's . . . '

'Family.'

'She's not my family.'

'Well, she's mine. I wouldn't be eating if not for her.'

'She's done little for me.'

'You mean she hasn't financed your gambling. If she'd done that, you'd care very little about her personal preferences. The truth is, you don't like May because she's not a woman you can twist around your little finger.'

'I'll ignore that, Bella. All I want you to think about is that if you were sensible, you could be married to a very powerful man. You have the beauty and the brains.'

Bella's eyes widened as realisation took hold. She remembered Andrew saying that he had some business with Griffiths.

'Is that what all this is about? Griffiths?'

'He's very taken with you.'

'The feeling isn't mutual.'

'You know, people in our position seldom marry for love. That comes much later.'

'I can promise you, I will never love

Mister Griffiths, now or later.'

'That's such a pity, because he asked me and I said I'd approach you on his behalf.'

'In that case, it's a definite no. I would never marry a man who didn't have the courage to tell me how he felt himself, instead of using my brother as a medium.'

'Let's put that aside for now, dearest. You probably just need time to get used to the idea.' Andrew tied the reins to the buggy, but made no move to get down. 'Bella, you haven't told anyone the truth have you?'

'The truth?'

'You know. About the vineyard.'

'No. I don't know if May knows, but she hasn't said anything.'

'Good, because I'd rather people didn't know. A man has to keep some pride, especially around here.'

'I told you before we came that it makes no difference to me.'

'Well it wouldn't, would it? After all . . . '

There was a low cough behind them.

Bella turned in her seat to see Vance standing at the side of the buggy.

'Good evening.'

'Good evening,' she whispered, wondering how much he had heard. 'You have a dreadful habit of sneaking up on people,' she said lightly, forcing a smile. It hurt her to realise that she enjoyed her time in America much more when her brother was absent.

'It must be my pedigree,' he said, glancing at Andrew. Bella's heart hung heavily in her chest. So he had heard. 'Here, let me help you down.'

He lifted her from the buggy in one easy movement, his strong hands warm through the thin fabric of her gown.

'You look very nice tonight, Miss Tennyson.'

Bella wondered why she had suddenly become Miss Tennyson to him. He let her go so quickly it was as if she had burned his hands.

'Thank you . . . Mister Eagleson,' she said, not sure if she wanted to cry. Did he think she was as bigoted as her

90

brother? 'You look very nice too.'

He wore a black suit, with a crisp white shirt with a black shoestring tie. He stood head and shoulders above every other man in the vicinity.

'So,' said Andrew, who had climbed down from the buggy and walked around to them. 'When are we going to meet the lucky lady, Vance?' He seemed unaware that he had caused offence. Or, thought Bella sadly, perhaps he did not care.

'Gloria is coming soon, I hope. Your sister has kindly agreed to put her up for a while.'

'Well, that's wonderful. I'm sure we'll all be great friends. Now if you two will excuse me, I need to find Mister Griffiths. I don't suppose you'd be kind enough to escort my sister the rest of the way?'

'I'm honored you trust her to me,' said Vance, through tight lips.

'Of course I do. You're a good friend, Vance. I was just saying so to Bella a moment ago.'

Bella cringed at Andrew's patronising tone. She wished he would hurry up and leave them alone. When he saw Arthur Griffiths in the distance, he did just that.

'I'm sorry,' she whispered to Vance, when Andrew was out of earshot.

'You don't have to apologise for your brother. I told you that.'

'I know but his behaviour in a saloon is one thing. The way he spoke about you is another.' She looked up at him with large, sad eyes. 'Why did you call me Miss Tennyson? I thought we were friends.'

'We are, but maybe your brother is right. Maybe your association with me isn't a good thing.'

'I don't care what others think,' said Bella. 'I just don't want us to be awkward with each other. You're one of the few people I can trust here.'

'But your brother wouldn't let you marry me.' Vance sounded bitter, but also tired, as if this insult was one he'd had to swallow too many times.

'Surely the discussion is academic since you're engaged to Gloria,' she said, trying hard to smile.

He reached up and stroked her cheek. 'And what would you say, Bella? If I did ask.'

They seemed to stand there for an age, whilst he waited for her to answer. She wanted to say 'oh yes', to tell him that she would be proud to be his wife, and that since the day she'd met him she'd lain awake at night thinking about him, and what it might feel like to be in his arms. To do so would be to lay herself bare, and she could not do that. Not knowing that he was in love with someone else.

'But you wouldn't because you're in love with Gloria, so I think it's best if we don't discuss it. Don't you?'

'I think I just got my answer,' he said, his face darkening. He turned and walked away from her. After a few feet, he stopped and turned back. 'Come on.' He held out his arm. 'I promised your brother I would escort you to the dance, and I never break my promises, Miss Tennyson.'

Bella took his arm meekly, more miserable than she had ever felt. Her reply seemed to have convinced him that she felt the same way as her brother, but what else could she have said? After all, he had not made a proper marriage proposal. He had been talking hypothetically. If only she could have answered in the same way, but for Bella there was nothing hypothetical about her feelings for Vance Eagleson.

The rest of the evening passed pleasantly enough. The Petersons were good hosts, insisting everyone ate well from the buffet of fried chicken, spare ribs and potato salad. The dancing, for Bella, was exhilarating, and a million miles away from the sedate tea dances she attended in England. People whooped and cheered, whilst following what to Bella sounded like impossible instructions from the leader of the band.

When a young man approached her and asked her to dance, she looked around for Vance but he was deep in conversation with Mr Peterson and another man, whilst a young woman hung on his arm looking up at him with doe eyes. So Bella allowed herself to be led to the dance floor.

'You'll have to translate for me,' she said to her partner.

'Heck, ma'am, I don't have a clue what they say most of the time. I just follow everyone else.' So that was what they did, sometimes getting tangled up in a sea of arms. No one seemed to mind. Everyone behaved with informal abandon. It was exhausting but exhilarating for Bella.

Andrew was a great hit with the young women, who all adored his accent. Bella was asked to dance many times after the first young man approached her, but never by Vance. He drew his own circle of admirers.

'You must tell us all about your great-grandfather,' one young lady purred as she clutched his arm. Bella was waiting to get a drink of punch and

Vance and the girl had approached the table. 'Was he really a savage?'

'It depends what you mean by savage,' said Vance, not seeming in the least bit offended by the crass question. 'All men are savages when stripped to the bone.'

'Why, marshal, I do believe you are the most provocative man I've ever had the pleasure of meeting.'

'Yes, but would your brother let me marry you?' said Vance.

Bella froze, her glass mid-air.

'I don't have a brother, and Daddy lets me do whatever I want.'

'Unfortunately,' said Bella, in icy tones, 'the marshal is already spoken for. Which is a great loss for the ladies of Milton.'

'All is fair in love and war,' said the young woman, clearly besotted.

'Be careful, Miss Grant,' said Vance. 'You'll be leading me astray.'

'Oh, I do hope so,' said Miss Grant.

Bella slammed down her glass and walked away. A waltz had just started and she found herself standing alone in the middle of the dance floor, not knowing which way to turn, whilst others danced around her. Suddenly a hand caught hers. It was Vance.

'We'd better start dancing before they run us over,' he said, putting his hand on her waist.

They began to move in time to the music. The singer was lamenting about a rather accident-prone girl called Clementine.

Bella could feel her heart beating fast as Vance held her close, his body against hers, taut and strong. They danced for a while, until the ice between them began to thaw. She would have gladly spent the whole evening in his arms. There were other good-looking men at the dance, but Vance eclipsed them all.

'I'm sorry,' he whispered against her hair. His warm breath brushed her neck. 'I shouldn't have said all those things.'

'Then why did you? To impress Miss Grant.'

'No, because you didn't give me the

answer I wanted.'

'You're engaged to someone else.'

'And that upsets you?'

'It's none of my business,' said Bella. It hurt her to breathe, thinking of him being with Gloria.

'One day I'll persuade you to tell me how you really feel.'

'Please don't play games with my heart, Vance. Unlike Miss Grant, I'm not experienced enough with men to know how to respond in kind.'

He brushed the centre of her palm with his thumb, causing a thrill to charge through her body. 'Being responsive to a man is more than about knowing what to say,' he whispered. 'Miss Grant there would run a mile yelling 'savage' if I touched her the way I just touched you.'

'I'm only staying because we're in the middle of a dance and it would be rude for me to walk away,' said Bella. As much as she tried to be angry with him, she found his closeness intoxicating. It would suit her if the dance lasted forever.

'Would you run if I kissed you?'

'I'd probably slap your face.' Bella was not quite sure that was true, but she tried to say it and mean it, which she felt was at least something.

'Really?' He grinned. 'You'd slap my face?'

'Yes, really.'

'But you're such a polite little English girl. Surely you'd just faint.'

'You appear to be confusing me with some other little English girl,' said Bella. 'If you behaved like a cad, I'd be forced to slap you.'

He threw back his head and laughed at that. 'A cad? What a quaint old word.' He put his mouth nearer to her, until she felt his lips brushing her cheek lightly. 'Believe me, the way I feel right now, you'd be yelling 'savage' not 'cad'.'

'No,' said Bella looking up at him with earnest eyes. 'I'd never say that to you, Vance.'

'May I cut in?' Griffiths appeared at the side of them.

To Bella's dismay, Vance stood aside,

almost as if it were a relief to let her go. 'Of course.'

If it had been possible for Bella to dance with Griffiths whilst standing in a separate field, she would have done it. As such she kept as much distance as she could between herself and him.

'You look very beautiful tonight, Miss Tennyson. Or may I call you Bella?' He did not wait for an answer. 'Your brother has told me so much about you. I wondered if I might call on you sometime?'

'I'm very sorry, Mister Griffiths. I don't know what my brother has said, but I am not looking for a husband.'

'Really? The way you were dancing with the marshal, folks might be forgiven for thinking otherwise.'

Bella pulled away. 'Thank you, Mister Griffiths, but I'm very tired. I'd like to go home now.'

'Then allow me to escort you.'

'That won't be necessary. My brother will . . . ' Bella looked around for Andrew, and saw him far in the distance, riding the buggy towards Milton. It meant she had no means of getting home.

'I told him I would see you home safely.'

'Thank you, but I can find my own way home.' Bella turned away, trying to look more resolute than she felt. She walked to the corral, but most of the guests had started to leave, and those that remained she did not know well enough to ask for assistance.

She sat down on the edge of a water trough, and rested her head in her hands. She was miles from home, and had no transport, but she was not going to be left at the mercy of Arthur Griffiths. She could hardly believe Andrew would put her in such a compromising position. Did he really expect her to prostitute herself? She wondered exactly what Griffiths had promised him in return for handing her over like a bag of wheat from the supply store.

'Bella? I saw your brother leave. Is he

coming back for you?' Vance's deep tones came from somewhere above her. She looked up to see him astride his horse. He had removed his jacket, his white shirt standing out like a beacon of light in the darkness. She shook her head.

'No, I don't think so. And Griffiths . . . ' She shuddered.

'Come on, I'll take you home.'

She took the hand he offered without hesitation, and he pulled her up so that she sat in front of him, sitting sideways.

Neither said anything for the first mile or so. He had his arms around her waist, holding onto the reins. She could feel the heat of his skin beneath his shirt. She had to fight the temptation to lay her head against his chest, but she was acutely aware of his body brushing against the side of her breast. She shivered a little but it was not an unpleasant feeling.

'Are you cold, Bella? You're trembling.'

How could she tell him that he was

the one making her tremble? The very nearness of him was enough to send her senses into a tailspin. Andrew had said that he was sure she would not do anything immoral, yet Bella knew that if Vance were to ask her, she would do anything he wanted. As Miss Grant had said, Gloria was not here.

'Do you like Miss Grant?' asked Bella, trying to turn the conversation away from the way her body was reacting to him. The annoyance that Miss Grant had caused her was enough for her to use it as a barrier between herself and Vance.

'No, she's a little too vacuous for my tastes. Does it bother you to think I might?' he asked her.

'It's really none of my business,' said Bella. 'Though I'm sure Gloria would . . .'

Vance stopped the horse and pulled Bella into his arms. He turned her face towards him, covering her mouth with his. She should have fought him off. It would have been the right thing to do. But all thoughts of right and wrong disappeared under the urgency of his kiss, and the feel of his hands on her body.

'Now tell me how you feel about Miss Grant,' he muttered savagely, covering her neck with kisses and tracing the curve of her breast with his fingertips. She moaned, running her fingers through his thick hair, wanting his hands to cover every part of her.

'I hate her,' said Bella. She could not speak any more because his lips found hers again. He caressed her mouth with the tip of his tongue, sending an electric flame shooting through her body. Bella's only previous experience of kissing had involved a chaste kiss on the cheek by one of her beaus in England, and that was after six months of discussing the weather in the parlour. Nothing had prepared her for a man as experienced as Vance. He knew how to kiss her and exactly how and where to touch her. She was both terrified and exhilarated by the feelings he aroused in her.

It was probably just as well that her fear was stronger than she was at that time. 'No,' she said, pulling away. 'We can't.'

Vance leaned back and took a deep breath, leaving Bella feeling more than a little disappointed. If truth be known, she wanted him to go on kissing her. But he was an honourable man, and despite her disappointment, she loved him even more for behaving as an honourable man should.

'You're right. I'm sorry. I shouldn't have done that.' He got off the horse and walked a few feet away, looking up at the diamond-strewn sky, as if seeking some advice from above. Bella sat in silence, whilst he stared into the distance, seeming to be bringing his emotions and his customary stillness back in check. 'I promise it won't happen again, Miss Tennyson.'

He walked alongside the horse the rest of the way, leaving Bella to sit in the saddle. She felt cold and alone. More than once she fought the compulsion to lean forward and stroke his hair.

She told herself it was probably for the best. She knew that if he kissed her again she would not be able to say no. Vance was a man who kept his promises. Had he not said so? It was with sinking heart that Bella realised he would probably be true to his word.

When they were just half a mile from the vineyard a gunshot rang out in the night.

6

Vance pulled her from the horse, and threw her to the ground, covering her body with his, whilst his one hand struggled to get his gun out of its holster. Another two or three shots hit the area around them. The horse bolted, turning and running off towards Milton.

Vance fired in the direction of one of the shots, but whether it found its target, it was hard to tell. He hauled Bella up roughly and pulled her behind a large rock.

'What's happening?' she whispered, suppressing the urge to cry out.

'We're being shot at.'

'Yes, I'd worked that out, but why?' she asked, trying to keep hidden.

'I think it's likely that I'm being shot at. Obviously Milton is already tired of its new marshal.'

The reality of their situation hit Bella like one of the rocks on the ground. She began to shiver, and this time it was not a result of Vance's proximity.

'The vineyard is less than half a mile away,' he said. 'I want you to run there now . . .'

'I'm not leaving you.'

'Bella, they don't want you, they want me. So I think you'll be safe. Just keep to this side of the canyon, using the rocks for cover. Then fetch help.'

'Help? Who? There's only May.'

'Yes, and she's pretty good with a gun, and I'm gonna run out of bullets soon. So will you please go fetch her?'

'I don't want to leave you,' said Bella, torn between wanting to fetch help and wanting to stay at his side. 'What if they kill you while I'm gone?'

'What if they kill us both when you stay?'

'I'd rather that than you die out here alone.'

Another shot rang through the air, close enough to suggest that whoever was firing had worked out their position. Bella and Vance ducked further down behind the rock, but it afforded them scant protection.

'Bella, you're no help to me here. In fact, I'd say you were a hindrance the way you keep talking all the time. So please, will you go? Crawl to that next rock, then the next one . . . '

Even though it hurt her to admit it, Bella knew he was right. Her being there only made things worse. Vance would probably die trying to protect her. Still, the thought of leaving him to be killed tore at her heart.

'I'll bring help,' she said.

She started crawling to the next rock, only to have a bullet hit the ground near to her hand. She felt Vance yank her backwards. 'They can see your white dress,' he said. 'Damn! I should have thought of that.'

'You said they didn't want to shoot me.'

'They don't, but I'm wearing a white shirt. They won't know if it's me or you so they'll just shoot anyway. Damn, damn, damn!' He leaned against the rock, but a sudden footfall caused him to spin around and fire. They heard a cry in the night.

'Well, it sounds like I hit one,' he said. 'Now we need to find somewhere to take cover.' He looked around him. 'I know where we can go.'

He picked up a couple of pebbles and threw them to his right, before pulling Bella to the left, and the next rock along. She heard another shot fire out, presumably in the direction of the pebbles.

'There's some caves up in the canyon,' he said in a low voice. 'We'll try and get up there.'

'Won't we be trapped?'

'Yes, but there's a few of them and they're dark and deep. Come on.'

It took them over half an hour of moving slowly, from rock to rock, whilst Vance worked at redirecting the rein of fire from their assailants. Finally, they reached a ledge in the canyon and another rock to hide behind.

'Be careful up here,' he said. 'Keep very low, because we'll be in view. Wait a minute. I've got a better idea.' He took off his shirt and rolled it up tight. His dark skin tone camouflaged well against the rocks. 'Now we only have to worry about your dress.'

'I am not taking it off.'

'No, if you do that, I'll be more of a danger to you than they are. I know . . . ' He picked up a handful of dirt and brushed it on the skirt.

'This is my best dress.'

'You've got a choice, Bella. It can either be stained with dirt or blood. Perhaps you'd rather deal with the bodice.'

She picked up some dirt and began rubbing it over her dress.

'Turn around, so I can get the back.'

Bella did as she was told, trying hard not to think about his hands sweeping dirt over her rear.

'May is going to be furious,' she said.

'Not when I bring you home alive,

she isn't. Come on.'

He led her across the ledge. At first it was wide, and they were able to take cover behind some of the rocks that rested on the edge. Then it became narrower, with cover hard to come by. He missed out the first cave, and the second, pulling her around a corner where the ledge became narrower still.

'Don't look down,' said Vance, with his back to the ledge. Bella did the exact opposite, feeling herself sway a little. She grabbed the cliff wall, and cried out in terror.

'Shh,' said Vance as a shot rang out, eager to hide their position.

He held her hand tightly, before leading her into a third cave. When they'd walked a bit further inside, any light from the moon and stars disappeared, leaving them in pitch blackness. Bella walked forward a little, coming straight up against Vance's bare chest. She moved, backing into a wall, which felt damp and slimy to the touch.

'With any luck they'll get tired of

looking in the other caves and give up.'

'What if they don't?'

'They won't be able to enter the cave with their guns pointed, not on that narrow ledge. They'll be too busy holding on to the side, so I'll be waiting to pick them off with mine. Are you cold?'

'I'm freezing.'

'Here.' He reached out in the dark. 'Put my shirt on.'

'What about you?'

'I'll be fine. Put it on. It'll be better for both of us if you do.'

Bella, not wanting to ask what he meant by that, put the shirt on. It was still warm from where he'd worn it, and smelled of him.

Using the wall to guide her, she sat down on the ground, her legs suddenly very weak. She didn't know if that was from the fear or Vance's nearness — she could feel him very close to her, joining her on the ground, leaning against the opposite wall — but either way, her legs would no longer hold her weight.

'Are you all right, Bella?'

'Yes. No. I've never been shot at before, nor had a man rub dirt all over my best dress.'

'I'm glad to hear it.'

'How long do you think we'll have to stay here, Vance?'

'I don't know. Maybe when my horse gets back to town, they'll realise something is wrong and come looking for us.'

'But they won't know where to look.'

'They'll find us. Don't worry.'

She felt him move slowly in the darkness, then his shoulder nudged against hers.

'Sorry,' he said, 'it's cold in here. I thought we could share some body heat. Who knows how long we'll be here.'

'Have your shirt back.'

'No, you wear it. It looks better on you.'

'You can't even see me.'

'In my imagination it looks better on you.'

114

Outside they heard small stones falling from the ledge.

'Shh.'

She heard him cock his gun, and waited, hardly daring to breathe.

Suddenly a voice called out in the night. 'Are you sure this was the way they came?'

'That's Bill,' whispered Bella.

'Shh . . .'

'Yes.' The second voice came from further away. 'I'm sure of it.'

More stones fell, and Bill swore out loud. 'The boss didn't say nothing about climbing the canyon,' he said. Half of his back came into view in the mouth of the cave, but it did not seem as if he noticed the cliff face had ended. 'I hate heights. Where are you? Are you coming up?'

When Bill lurched forward, nearly falling to his death, Bella gasped, which was followed by Vance clamping his hand over her mouth. It was lucky for Bella that Bill's own cry in the night covered her own. Bill scrambled for purchase on the ledge.

'Hell, I'm coming down,' he said, moving back the way he came and out of sight. 'Before I kill myself. I didn't sign up for this.'

After a few minutes of waiting and watching, Vance got up and moved towards the entrance, keeping his gun aloft. He looked out to either side, before coming back to sit next to Bella.

'They've gone. Now we just have to hang out here until we're sure they're not waiting at the bottom of the canyon.'

★   ★   ★

It was morning when Bella opened her eyes. The sunrise shone into the cave, lighting up their hiding place, and bringing much needed heat. She moved her head to find that she was using Vance's bare chest as a pillow, her hand resting on his flat belly. His skin felt smooth against her cheek and fingertips. She traced the line of his torso with her fingertips, from his navel up to his chest, feeling her excitement rising. She stroked his nipple with the tip of her finger, fighting the urge to follow it with a kiss.

His hand clamped over hers. In less than a second he flipped over, and pinned her to the floor of the cave, with the weight of his body holding her down. He shifted slightly and her eyes widened as she became very aware of the effect her touch had on him.

'Vance . . . '

Before she could say another word he kissed her, pulling her body roughly up to him with one hand on her back, whilst the fingers of his other hand searched for the bottom of her dress, and began to slide up past her stockings to the silky skin of her thigh, sending darts of pleasure shooting through her. She raked her fingers along his bare back and answered his kiss with one full of longing.

'Marshal! Marshal! Are you up there?'

Vance pulled away, and dropped Bella like a stone. 'They've found us,' he said. 'You go first.'

'Why?' Bella's breath came quickly. She straightened her clothing, beginning to feel the weight of her shameless behaviour.

'Because if you don't, I'm going to ignore them and finish what we just started.' He took a deep breath. 'No. Give me my shirt. I'll go and speak to them, then when we've gone, you make your way home.'

'Why?' she asked again.

'Because if they find out you're here, they're going to start wondering exactly what we've been doing here all night. It'll ruin your reputation.'

He put on his shirt and made to leave the cave. Before he did, he turned back with a heart-wrenching smile. 'Next time you touch a man like that, you'd better be willing to deal with the consequences, because there might not be a deputy on hand to save you.'

It was early evening when Bella woke up in her own bed. She had spent the morning working, avoiding May's searching glances. The explanation she gave did not sound plausible, even to her. In the end, she feigned tiredness and sought the privacy of her bedroom. She must have been genuinely tired, because the next thing she knew dusk was falling and she heard shouting outside.

She jumped out of bed and went to the window. Griffiths stood looking down over the vineyard. Tom and Bill were hammering at the door of the bunkhouse, ordering Shen and the other Chinese workers to come out. Shen opened the door. The murderous look in his eyes caused Bill and Tom to step back momentarily, before they regained equilibrium and ordered him out using the most abusive language Bella had ever heard.

Tom wore a bandage around his arm, which Bella presumed was a result of being shot by Vance.

Wearing her dressing gown, and with her hair tousled around her head, Bella ran downstairs and out of the front door, closely followed by May coming from the parlour.

'What on earth is going on?' asked Bella, standing on the porch. She was surprised by how imperious her own voice sounded.

Griffiths turned and smiled. 'Good evening, Miss Tennyson. I'm sorry to have to tell you that you must leave this vineyard.'

'Leave?'

'Yes, you, Miss Tucker there and the workers. As I'm a gentleman, I'll give you and Miss Tucker till the morning to pack.' His voice became oily. 'Of course, we could come to an understanding where you remain.'

'Don't you worry, Miss Bella,' said May. 'I'll chase them off. Darn it, I left my gun in the kitchen. Varmints, catching a lady unawares like this.'

'I've no intentions of leaving here,'

said Bella. She held back May who had decided to put up her fists instead. 'What gives you the right to order us off our own property?'

Griffiths paused. 'Of course, I've been very remiss not to explain my presence here.' He reached into his pocket. 'Last night, your brother and I got into a game of cards. He ran out of money and no one else would lend him any. So he wrote this IOU. It gives me permission to take possession of the vineyard, and everything on it.'

Bella pulled her dressing gown tight, not liking the way Griffiths looked her up and down as he said those last few words. May nudged her slightly and pointed to the approach. Vance was riding towards them. Just the sight of him gave Bella more courage.

'I'm afraid that won't be possible, Mister Griffiths,' said Bella defiantly, looking him in the eye.

'It's more than possible, Miss Tenny-son. I won it fair and square.'

'I'm afraid not,' she said. She spoke

slowly, to allow Vance more time to reach them. He appeared to understand and speeded up on seeing Griffiths and his men. Bella hesitated. Andrew would be furious with her, but he should never have put her in this position. 'You see, Mister Griffiths, the vineyard does not belong to my brother. Aunt Bella left it to me. The deeds are in my name.'

Griffiths' face turned pale. 'What?'

'The vineyard belongs to me, not to my brother. He didn't want people to know . . . ' Bella stopped. Her brother's pride seemed irrelevant, and she did not want to enter into further discussion with Griffiths. 'I really am surprised you failed to check.'

'I just assumed . . . '

'Yes, as most people did, I'm sure,' said Bella. 'But my aunt believed in women owning property. Now, Mister Griffiths, I would like you and your men to leave my land.'

Bill and Tom seemed to realise more rapidly than Griffiths that they were in a difficult position, not least because whilst Bella had been talking Shen and the other workers surrounded them.

'This isn't over,' said Griffiths. 'It's a matter of honour.'

'No,' said Vance, 'it's a matter of law, and you know as well as I do that a man cannot pledge something that does not belong to him.'

'I wouldn't push your luck if I were you, marshal. You never know what might happen one night when you're travelling home.'

Bella felt an icy chill run up her spine. So Griffiths had been behind the attack last night.

'Like the last two marshals, you mean,' said Vance. 'Maybe you'd better hire someone who can shoot a moving target in the dark.' He nodded towards Bill and Tom.

'I had nothing to do with that,' said Griffiths. His voice had become low, dangerous. 'I mean with the last two marshals. I heard you were ambushed last night. It just so happens my men were both up country doing some work for me. I've got the paperwork to prove it. It took them all night. Not that anyone would cry over your loss.' He glanced up at Bella, with an evil gleam in his eye. 'Well, not for long if I had anything to do with it.'

Bella gasped as Vance jumped from his horse and went to stand eye to eye with Griffiths, though with his height it was more a case of Vance's eye to Griffiths' forehead.

'Like I said, a man cannot pledge what doesn't belong to him. That includes his sister. Now you run along and leave Miss Tennyson to go about her business, before I take you in for trespassing and have those two men arrested for trying to kill us.'

Griffiths seemed to think about it for a long time, his hand hovering over his gun belt. The air was thick with tension, and Bella could hear May breathing heavily next to her.

'Come on, Griffiths, you won't get your hands dirty,' said Vance. 'At least not with witnesses.' Vance turned to Bella.

'Shall I arrest him now for trespassing?'

'Yes, lock him up,' said May. 'Him and his no good men.' She cast a hateful glance at her brother.

'No,' said Bella. 'Just make them leave.' Later she would regret not saying yes, but at the time she had no hint of the heartache to come.

'This isn't over,' said Griffiths, as he got onto his horse and rode away. The workers stepped aside to let Bill and Tom leave, jostling them as they did so. Griffiths' men got on their horses and followed him.

Vance called Shen over and had a quiet conversation with him. Shen nodded, before relaying the conversation to one of the younger workers. The young Chinese man got onto his horse and rode off at breakneck speed towards Milton.

'Thank you,' Bella said to Vance, when everything fell silent. May had made herself scarce, muttering something about cooking up a mess of beans for everyone. 'I'm glad you were here.'

'It's my job.'

'But that's not why you came,' said Bella.

'No. Would you walk with me a moment?'

Bella tied her dressing gown tighter, and walked alongside him in the vineyard. It was already starting to show the benefits of Shen's expertise, with much of the excess growth pruned back. Vance was in a serious mood and said nothing for a while.

'What is it?'

'I'm leaving.'

'You've only just arrived,' said Bella, trying to sound light-hearted.

'No, I'm leaving Milton. Not for good. I need to go and see Gloria. I have to talk to her.'

'Yes, of course.' Bella had dreaded this moment, but she fought hard to regain her composure. 'I suppose it's about last night.'

Vance stopped and turned to her. 'Of course it's about last night. And this morning. Damn it, Bella . . . '

'I know, but you've nothing to be ashamed of. Nothing happened.'

'I still need to see Gloria. To tell her.'

'Is that wise?' questioned Bella. She wanted to make it easier for him, to take away the pain in his eyes. 'It was just a kiss brought about by too much punch, the moonlight ride and being stuck together in tense circumstances. That's all. There's no need to ruin your whole life because of it.'

'Is that all it was?' asked Vance.

'Yes. Wasn't it?' She wanted him to say no, to tell her that he wanted her as much as she wanted him. She longed to be in his arms, feeling his mouth on hers and his hands caressing her as they had that morning. But she also wanted him to be happy. He was a good man, and his need to go to see Gloria suggested to Bella that despite what happened between them, he really loved his fiancée.

'I guess it was.' He took a deep breath.

'When do you leave?'

'I was going to wait until next week, but I think the sooner the better. I'll go tomorrow.'

He left her standing alone in the vineyard. She lasted until he got onto his horse and rode out of sight before she ran back to the house and fell sobbing onto her bed.

* * *

Things were to get much worse. After lunch the following day, when Bella was working in the vineyard, Vance returned, riding his buggy up the approach. Her heart leapt. He had said he was leaving, but here he was. It took her a few moments to realise he was not alone. One of his deputies sat alongside him. She walked through the vineyard to meet them. Their faces were solemn.

'Vance, what is it?'

He jumped down from the buggy, and his deputy did likewise. They both walked around to the back.

'Bella . . . ' Vance seemed to have

shrunk in stature, with his shoulders hunched and his head down, barely able to make eye contact with her. 'Bella, I'm sorry, but we didn't get to him in time.'

'To who? You didn't get to who?'

'Shen's boy tried to warn Andrew to get out of town, to lie low for a while. He wouldn't listen to reason. He couldn't see the danger. Where's May. I think she should be here. May!'

'What? For goodness' sake, Vance. Tell me.'

'It's your brother. He's been shot in the back.'

The deputy threw back a blanket, to reveal Andrew lying dead on the back of the buggy. Bella screamed in shock, then clambered up onto the cart. He was pale, but looked as if he might only be sleeping.

'Andrew, Andrew, dearest, please wake up,' said Bella, taking him in her arms. 'Please wake up.' She was vaguely aware of shouting from the house, and people running out towards the cart.

'Bella, darling, come away,' said Vance. 'Come on.'

'You leave him alone. He's my brother,' she cried, throwing Vance's hand from her. 'Don't you touch him.'

Vance stepped back as if he had been slapped. May arrived and quickly took the situation in hand, climbing onto the cart with Bella.

'Come on, baby. Come to me,' she said. Bella turned and was about to push May away. Instead she fell into her arms, sobbing inconsolably.

'Take care of her, May,' Vance said. 'She won't let me.'

Bella protested loudly when they tried to pull her off the cart, collapsing in sobs as soon as they managed to wrench Andrew from her arms.

She came to her senses sitting on the chair in the parlour, with May tending her. Vance and the deputy stood with their backs to the hearth. They were talking in quiet tones with Shen, who was agreeing to make all the arrangements for Andrew's burial.

'Have you arrested Griffiths?' Bella asked, when her head had cleared.

'There's no proof he did it,' said Vance.

'But you know he did!'

'Knowing it and proving it are two different things, Bella. We're doing all we can. But your brother owed money all over town. I'm sorry, but Griffiths wasn't the only one with reason to . . . '

'No!' Bella stood up. 'No, that's not true. Andrew was a good man. He made mistakes, but . . . it must have been Griffiths. I want you to arrest him.'

'We can't unless we have proof. There were no witnesses when your brother was shot, but there are a dozen men can say they saw Griffiths playing poker in the saloon when it happened.'

'We know Griffiths has got a motive,' said the deputy. 'He was mightily upset that your brother lied to him about owning the vineyard.'

Bella fell back into the chair as realisation hit her. If she had not told

Griffiths the truth, then Andrew would still be alive. It was all her fault.

'I should have given it to him,' she whispered, a huge tear splashing from her cheek. 'I should have let Griffiths take the vineyard. Then Andrew would still be alive.'

'Would you be included in that deal?' said Vance, savagely.

'If it meant my brother would be standing here alive, yes,' said Bella, before her body became racked with sobs. May held her in her arms.

'There baby, let it all out now. I think you should go for now, marshal.' May turned to Vance. 'I'll take care of her.'

Vance hesitated, his face a mask of some emotion Bella could not name. 'Fine. Come on,' he said to his deputy. 'Shen, will you . . . '

'Yes, don't worry. I will take care of everything as you asked.'

'Thank you. If she needs anything, let me know.'

7

Life was such that Bella could not afford to cry for long. There was work to be done. She pulled herself together and got up every morning ready to face another day. It helped take her mind off Andrew's death.

A few days after Andrew's burial, Vance called over. Bella let him come to her this time, afraid to hear any more bad news.

'I just came to say goodbye,' he said.

'You're leaving? With Griffiths out there, killing people? You're leaving?'

'Griffiths has gone up country to take care of his other business interests. The deputies here are good men. They can manage whilst I'm gone. I'm only sorry you think I've let you down somehow.'

'No, it's not your fault,' she said, exhausted with grief. 'It's my fault.'

'You told Griffiths the truth. It was

something your brother should have done from the start.'

'So he deserved to die?'

'That's not what I said. What I mean is that you can't spend your life blaming yourself for Andrew's death. Or me for not arresting Griffiths.'

'Oh, don't worry. I know how it works. He's a powerful man around here. He can do pretty much what he wants.'

'Is that what you think? That I've been bought by Griffiths?'

'What I mean is that you're an out-sider, like me, so you have to be careful. After all, you don't want to get shot in the back, do you?'

'So now I'm a coward. Okay, I get that you're angry. I even understand why you are. But don't do this.'

'Do what?'

'Don't push away everyone who cares about you. May said you don't eat, you don't sleep, and you barely talk. Shen came all the way down to town yesterday just to tell me how worried he is about you. That's why I came up here today. I could have left without saying anything, but they're concerned about you.'

'I'm perfectly all right. I told you when we first met that English women are tougher than you think.'

'You're not that tough, Bella.' Vance caught her by the shoulders and for a moment she thought — hoped — he would kiss her. 'You have to stop this anger and bitterness. It's not you.'

'You don't know me!' she cried. 'I'm not little miss perfect. That's what Andrew called me. He was so angry with me, when Aunt Bella left me the vineyard, and I promised him, I promised I would never tell. He hated being dependent on me. That's why he did the things he did. He had to pretend that he was the one in control. That's why he lied to Griffiths too, and if I hadn't opened my big mouth, he might still be alive. So please don't tell me I can't be angry and bitter. I damn well can.'

She pulled away from him, annoyed

with herself for how much she wanted him, even now. She craved the comfort of his arms, and for him to tell her that everything would be all right. That would never happen. He was engaged to someone else. Which made her angrier still, both with herself and with him.

'Go on, go away to the rabbit skinning Gloria if you must!'

To Bella's surprise that made Vance laugh. 'I'll be back in a week or two. We'll talk then.'

'I'm sure Gloria will be keeping you far too busy, what with planning your wedding and everything.'

'I'll speak to you when I return. Maybe you'll be ready to listen to me then because you sure as hell ain't listening now.' He turned and walked away.

★ ★ ★

She dealt with his absence by working even harder, staying out in the vineyard long after dark, and working by the light of the moon and a lantern that she carried with her. Her back ached, but not nearly as much as her heart. She had cried so much over Andrew's death, that she thought she had become numb.

The pain she felt on Vance's departure caught her by surprise. Several weeks passed, but if Bella had been asked to summarise what had happened in that time, she couldn't say. Life was a blur of working in the vineyard and restless nights where, on the few occasions she did sleep, she was plagued by bad dreams.

'Miss Bella.'

'Yes, Shen.' Bella stopped and stood up straight, her back feeling as if it would break under the strain. It was eight o'clock in the evening, and the sun had set an hour before. 'What is it?'

'Miss Bella, come on inside now, and rest. You put me and my boys to shame, out here working so hard whilst we eat and sleep.'

'You deserve your rest.'

'And so do you, Miss Bella. Miss Tucker sent me out to get you. She is concerned about you. She said you did not eat breakfast this morning, and that you hardly ate any lunch.'

'I'm not very hungry, Shen.'

'Then come and rest. Killing yourself out here is not going to help anyone, and it only puts off the pain for another day,' he said knowingly.

'Well, if I can keep putting it off, then it will never catch up with me,' said Bella, with a bitter smile.

'That is what I think, when I remember my wife. But it finds me when I least expect it, and then it is harder to deal with.'

'You miss her dreadfully, don't you?'

'Yes.'

'Perhaps I could help you bring her over. I could apply for her to come and work for me. Then you'd be together.'

'You would do that?'

'Of course I would. It isn't right to be apart from the person you love most in the world.'

'Thank you. It would mean the world to me to have her here.'

'That's settled. We'll go into Milton tomorrow and speak to the lawyer. I'll tell the authorities that I'm sponsoring her. I hate to say it but, being European, I'll probably have more luck than you. We should use the unfair system to our advantage, shouldn't we?'

'That's a good idea.'

'She'll need somewhere to live when she gets here.' The plan energised Bella, giving her something else to focus on. 'She can't possibly sleep in the bunkhouse. I'll have a word with Mr Peterson. He built nice homes for his workers. I'm sure if I ask him, he'd build you both a little cottage to live in.'

Bella could see it in her mind's eye, with roses around the door, and Shen and his wife sitting on the porch, living out their last years together. The image brought a lump to her throat. If she could not be happy, at least she could make someone else happy.

'You are doing so much for me, Miss Bella. Would it be wrong of me to ask for something more?'

'Not at all. What is it?'

'Will you come inside and eat, then get some rest?'

'Very well,' said Bella. 'Since we'll have so much to do over the next few months, I'll do as you ask.' She picked up Hector who had been scurrying at her feet. 'Come on, we've been ordered inside.'

'There she is,' said May, when Bella entered the kitchen. Shen's sons were sitting around the table eating. They greeted her with affection. 'What do you want, honey?' May asked. 'Do you want some steak? Or fried chicken? I've fried up some potatoes, too. Here, sit in my rocking chair. It'll be more comfortable. You can eat with your food on your knees. We ain't standing on ceremony here, are we boys?'

Bella sat down, and let the gentle sway of the rocking chair soothe her. 'Please don't fuss, May.' She closed her eyes and remembered her home in England. They had lived in a small village, just outside London, where everyone knew everyone else. She thought of their house, which was on the village green. They had to sell it to pay some of Andrew's gambling debts and the cost of the journey to America. Bella wondered if it were still empty and whether the local squire who bought it might rent it out to her. She pictured her room, which overlooked the square, and the few friends she had left behind. Life, despite Andrew's problems, had seemed simpler then. Here, in this wide-open country, she was out of her depth.

When she opened her eyes again, Shen's boys had gone. May sat at the table darning her socks.

'Did you have a good sleep, honey? I've kept your dinner warm.'

'How long did I sleep?'

'About an hour or so. It's what you needed. The boys said to say goodnight. They're good kids, Shen's sons, aren't they?'

'Yes, they're decent young men. May?'

'What, honey?'

'I've been thinking about going home.'

May put her sock down. 'You are home, honey.'

'You know what I mean. I'm exhausted and sad. I wondered if . . . well . . . if you could buy the vineyard from me. I won't ask much. Just enough for my fare home and enough to live on until . . .'

'Until what? What are you going to do in England? You've told me yourself that there's no way a young lady can earn a living.'

'I could take in mending. Or write.'

'And what do you think the marshal is going to say if he knows I just let you up and leave for England all on your own?'

'I doubt he cares very much,' said Bella sadly. 'He's going to be returning here a married man, May.'

'Now how did you work that out?'

'They're engaged and he's gone to meet her. The proper thing to do, if they're travelling together, would be to get married. I've thought about it a lot, and it seems to me that's why he's gone. I can't be here when he returns. I can't. I love him, May.' Bella put her elbows on her knees and rested her head in her hands.

'What happened that night up on the canyon?'

'Nothing.' Bella sat up again. 'I promise you, nothing happened.'

'Darn it, honey, I don't care if you did or if you didn't. I just wanna be sure that if you do run away from here you're not taking a bundle of other trouble with you. I'd never let you go if that were true. We'd work it out together, honey, you and I.'

Bella stood up and went to sit at the table. She reached out and put her hands over May's. 'I'm not having a baby if that's what you think. Nothing like that happened. At least, I mean, it didn't go that far.'

'So he kissed you then?'

'We kissed each other.'

'Well, what are you worrying about? If he kissed you it means he's got feelings for you. He won't marry Gloria.'

'He loves her May.'

'Honey, you're a smart young woman, but you haven't got a clue when it comes to men.'

'And you're an expert?' Bella raised an eyebrow.

'Well, maybe not, but I know how someone's eyes look when they could eat a person up like a plate of pancakes and syrup.'

'But men don't always love the women they kiss, do they? Look at the girls down at Aunt Kitty's.'

'They don't go to Aunty Kitty's for the kissing.'

'What do they go for?'

'I ain't talking to you about that sort of thing. Happen the marshal will teach you one day. Well some of it, anyway. Not all of it. I'd shoot him myself if he did that.'

'Not if he's married to another woman he won't. I'm not stealing another woman's husband, May, and neither do I intend being someone's mistress.'

'Bella, honey,' May took her hand. 'Forget about the marshal for a minute. When you came here, it was like mine and your Aunt Bella's baby girl had arrived. I know we're not blood relations, but I've come to feel like you're my own girl. You're hurting over Andrew's death and I know the marshal being gone is adding to that pain. But there's others here who love you and will take care of you. Me, Shen, the boys. We all think you're the cat's whiskers. Who have you got like that over in England?'

'I'm beaten, May. This country, it's won. Like the man said on the train, it'll drive a person mad. I can feel myself losing my grip.'

'Aw, honey, you just lost a loved one. Of course you're losing your grip. The only reason this country drives people mad is that those who come here don't learn that you gotta climb those mountains. You can't just stride right on over them. Your brother, God rest his soul, didn't learn that. I ain't saying it's easy, honey, and I ain't saying it won't break your back and your heart at times, when you think you've got so far up then something knocks you back down again. But you got it in you to reach the top. You just can't give up now.'

'It's such a hard climb, May,' said Bella. A tear rolled down her cheek.

'I know, honey, but you're making the mistake of thinking you gotta do it all alone. You've got me to pull you up. And Shen, and the boys.'

How could Bella tell May that as much as she loved them all, it was not their hands she wanted to see when she looked up?

'The marshal will be helping you too, if you just trust in him,' said May, who was even shrewder than Bella had given her credit for.

'He's going to be married to someone else, May.'

'It ain't over till it's over,' May said, sagely.

8

That night in Bella's dream, the ship pulled into an empty quayside and only she disembarked. As far as she could tell, she was the only passenger to have made the trip. No one waited for her as she walked down the gangplank. It came to her with a painful realisation that May had been right. She had no one in England. The gangplank slipped from under her the moment she put one foot onto the quay. She spun around to see the ship already starting its return journey. On the top deck, two people waved to her. She could not make out the woman's face, although she knew instinctively that this woman was more beautiful and more wonderful than she could ever be. She could tell that by the way the man kept his eyes on the woman as he waved goodbye to Bella.

'Vance,' she whispered. 'No, please, don't go.'

They drifted away into the distance, then the sky became ochre and the ship went up in flames. Suddenly she was back in the kitchen at the vineyard. May was baking a cake but when she took it out of the oven the fruit was burned. The aroma hit Bella's nostrils, sickly and sweet.

'Quick, honey,' shouted May. 'You've got to . . . ' The voice faded before Bella could make out what she said.

Did she say eat it? Bella thought that must be it. But she did not want to eat it. The cake was burned and it would taste awful.

'Honey, honey, you've got to wake up.'

'I am awake,' said Bella.

'Darn it, I can't wake her. I wonder if the smoke has got to her.'

'You shouldn't have burned the cake,' said Bella.

May took her by the shoulders and shook her roughly.

Bella's eyes snapped open. She was in her bedroom and judging by the red light shining through the windows, it appeared that the sun had risen. She could still smell the burning fruit.

'What is it?'

'Thank God,' said May. 'The vineyard is on fire. Get up, honey. Shen and the boys are trying to put out the flames, but we don't know how far it's going to spread.'

Bella rushed around looking for something to wear.

'There's no time for that, honey. Here's your dressing gown. We gotta get out of here now.'

They ran downstairs and out into the yard. The fire was on the left of them, near to the bunkhouse, and due to the direction of the breeze it was advancing on the building rapidly. Flames jumped and crackled, sending sparks up into the night sky.

'Shen and the boys?' asked Bella anxiously.

'They're okay, they've all got out.

They're round the back getting water from the pump.'

Bella was about to turn away and follow May to the approach when she saw a tiny head poking out from the bottom of the bunkhouse door. 'It's Hector!' She ran down the path.

'Honey, come on, you can't risk your own life just to save that darn rabbit. Bella, please, come back. Oh, damn that girl. I knew I should have killed that rabbit on the first day. Shen! Shen! We've got a problem.'

Bella could hear May shouting, but her only focus was in saving Hector. She had not let him live to have him cooked in a fire. Besides, he was one of the family now.

As she grew nearer to the bunkhouse she noticed something else. A foot sticking out from the end of the building, and the flames were getting closer to it. She ran to the side and saw by the light of the fire that the man had tripped and banged his head on a rock. It was Bill Tucker.

Whatever her private thoughts about him, and the fact that he had clearly been involved in setting fire to the vineyard, Bella knew she could not leave him there to die. Hector, she realised with an aching heart, would have to take his chances. She called for the others, and then tried to drag him out.

'Bella, honey, get out of there. You're gonna get burned.'

'May, it's your brother. He's been hurt.'

He was very heavy and it took her a few minutes just to move him a couple of feet. She could hear the others calling to her, the air becoming filled with a cacophony of shouting, but she was so intent on the task in hand she could not hear what they were saying. When she felt the heat on her back, she understood exactly why they had been shouting.

She dropped Bill to the ground and turned around. The breeze had sent the fire around in an arc, so that she was trapped in the centre. The only way to go was the direction of the bunkhouse, but there was no door on the other side, and she could no longer get around it. Only a few yards separated Bella and the fire, and she had nowhere to go.

She heard the others call something about blankets. Yes, that was a good idea. She ran into the bunkhouse and found a couple of blankets, draping one over Bill and the other around herself. Then she heard the others say something about water. She searched the bunkhouse again but there was no water. Only the moonshine that Shen and the workers drank. She doubted that would help, though if she were honest she would not have minded a drink of it to steady her nerves.

She came back out of the bunkhouse just in time to see the flames shoot higher and a large body, covered in a blanket from head to toe coming towards her. Whoever it was swooped her up. She realised the blanket was soaking wet, and at last understood that they had not been shouting instructions to her, but making plans to save her.

'What about Bill Tucker?' she cried.

'We'll do our best to come back for him. Right now I want you somewhere safe.'

'Vance?' Despite the circumstances, her heart gave a joyous leap.

'Hold on tight and cover your head, darling, it's gonna get a little warm.' With that, he hurtled through the flames and carried her to safety.

★ ★ ★

They pulled Bill Tucker out of the fire, but he did not regain consciousness. May tended him whilst Bella, Vance, Shen and the other workers ran from the pump with buckets of water, trying to stop the spread of the flames. The vineyard itself did not come right up to the front door, but there were shrubs and small trees along the pathway, all of which were brittle due to the hot, dry weather. All it needed was for some sparks to jump across and the house would be next.

After an hour others began to arrive from the canyon. Ike Peterson and his boys, Mr Grant and his cowhands. They formed a chain, bearing buckets of water from the pump at the back of the house to the fire at the front. They worked with silent determination.

Finally, as dawn was rising, the fire began to burn itself out. It had taken the bunkhouse, and several acres of the vineyard — it would be a while before they could ascertain the full extent of the damage — but due to some of the men digging a ditch running the length of the house, and filling it with water, it had stopped short of the porch. Smoke still billowed in the air, but it was thick and damp, more like fog.

Bella sat down on the steps of the porch, and Vance sat next to her. Shen and the other workers sat on the ground, passing around canteens of water, part drinking them and part pouring them over their heads. Ike

Peterson, Mr Grant and their people had waved them goodbye and returned home a few minutes earlier.

'All that work,' said Bella. 'Up in smoke.' Her eyes stung, but she did not know if they were tears of sadness or the effects of the smoke. Her emotions were so mixed up, it could be either. One thing she had realised, during the long night's work, was that she could never leave this place. It had taken nearly losing it to teach her how much she loved her home.

'It'll grow again,' said Vance.

May came from around the corner of the house, where she had been tending Bill, as far away from the fire as possible. Bella looked up, a question in her eyes. May shook her head and sat on the bottom step.

'I'm so sorry, dearest,' said Bella softly, reaching down and putting a hand on May's shoulder.

'I'm not,' said May. 'We could've died because of him. You shouldn't have risked your own life trying to save him, honey. He meant to kill us in our beds, Bella. And me his kin.'

'You wouldn't have left him there,' said Bella. 'You're a better person than that, May.'

'No, honey, you are. And we all love you for it.' May got up. 'I'm gonna go take a bath, then cook us all up some breakfast. We need to find somewhere for Shen and the boys to sleep.'

'They can sleep in the spare rooms, May. We'll get some wood and build a new bunkhouse. It'll be bigger and better.'

'Does this mean you're not going back to England?' asked May.

'Yes. I suppose it does.'

'You were planning to go home?' said Vance, when May had gone into the house.

'Yes. But not now. Thank you for your help last night. How did you know about the vineyard being on fire?'

'I was on my way up here when I saw the flames.'

'Coming out here? At three o'clock in

the morning? Is there something wrong in Milton?'

'Yep.'

'Oh no. What is it this time?'

He turned and looked at her intently, his face was smudged with smoke. 'You're not there.'

'Oh.' Bella shifted her gaze downwards. 'But Gloria is, I suppose. She came back with you, didn't she?'

Shen, who was watching the scene, muttered something to the other workers and they began to walk away.

'Where are you going?' asked Bella. 'You should get some rest.'

'We are going to wash in the creek, Miss Bella. Then we will come and get some food. You and the marshal have your talk.' Shen smiled, knowingly. Bella blushed as they walked away.

'You were saying about Gloria?' said Vance.

'That you brought her with you.'

'What made you think I was going to do that?'

'Because I thought that's why you

went. To bring her back to Milton. Didn't you?'

Vance leaned back onto the step and stretched out his long legs. 'I need to explain to you about Gloria.'

'You don't have to explain anything, Vance. I know you are engaged to be married. I knew that when we . . . I've always known,' she said sadly.

'You really think I'd have kissed you the way I did, if I was in love with another woman?'

'But you must have been in love with her. To want to marry her.'

'Bella, I'm sorry if I ever misled you over Gloria. We decided to marry because she wanted to please her father and I wanted to get back in with mine. They spent so much of our childhood expecting us to grow up and marry, we thought they'd be delighted. And they were. But we were never in love. It was a union that suited us both because at the time neither of us was in love with anyone else. Despite that, she still deserved to be treated with respect, so I went to see her to ask her to release me from my promise.' He sat up again and pulled Bella towards him. 'I told her all about you.'

'You did? What did you tell her?'

'About how I felt about you. That I fell in love with you the first moment I saw you.'

Bella jumped up off the step.

'What?' Vance stood up and took her arm. 'I'm sorry, I've obviously got things wrong.'

'Oh, you've got it very wrong,' said Bella.

'I see, you like me but you'd never marry a man like me, is that it?'

'I might have if you thought to ask me instead of going and telling another woman what you should be telling me first.'

'I asked you if you would marry me. Over at the Petersons'.'

'You were speaking hypothetically.'

'Bella, a man never speaks hypothetically about such things. If he did, he'd end up like one of those Mormons over

159

in Utah, with six or seven different wives.'

'You told Gloria how you felt about me before you even told me.'

'Damn it, I wanted to tell you, Bella, but after Andrew died you wouldn't let me, or anyone else, get close. You shut yourself off from everybody who cares about you. I was afraid that if I asked you then, you'd say no, because you were so angry with me for not preventing Andrew's death.'

'No, that's not true, Vance. I told you, it was my fault.'

He gently took her by the shoulders. 'It wasn't your fault. It was Andrew's fault. He was a grown man. An intelligent man, but also naïve in many ways. He underestimated Griffiths, because he was used to the English culture of fair play. I tried to warn him when he was in jail that night that it doesn't work like that out here, but he wouldn't listen to me. I even tried to tell him he was putting your life at risk, but he still ignored me. He thought he had it all under control. Andrew is not your fault, darling. He was damaged when he came here. This big old country just magnified the problems he already had.'

Bella turned away and looked at the fire damaged vineyard. 'I know.'

Everything Vance said was right. It was something she had known from the moment they set foot in America, far away in New York, after he found a card game within an hour of them disembarking. Andrew's problems were too deep, too entrenched for him to ever escape them. She spun back around. 'But that doesn't alter the fact that you chose to tell Gloria . . . '

Before she could say another word, Vance had her in his arms, kissing her. Five seconds into the kiss, she realised that it didn't matter about Gloria. Vance had come back to her just when she needed him most.

'I love you,' she said, when he reluctantly pulled away. 'I love you, and I would be honoured to be your wife,

161

Marshal Eagleson.'

She felt something brush her foot, and looked down. 'It's Hector!' She picked the rabbit up, and held him close. 'He's survived, Vance.'

When her tears finally began to fall, Vance was there to hold her close.

9

Bella thought that if there were any greater pleasure than standing on the porch watching a shirtless Vance helping Shen and the workers rebuild the bunkhouse, she had yet to find it. It had been a week since the vineyard fire, and despite the hard work ahead of her, Bella felt happier than she had ever been. The darkness seemed to have lifted, simply because Vance was back and he loved her. The only cloud, and one that seemed very far away, given her current joy, was Griffiths.

'I must admit,' said May, coming out onto the porch, and nodding over towards Vance, 'that if I was ever gonna choose a man, he'd be it.'

'Hands off,' said Bella, smiling. 'He's mine.'

'I told you, honey, it ain't over till it's over.' May winked. 'Nah, don't you worry. He adores you. At least I think that's the reason I have to force him to go home to Milton every night.'

'That won't always be so,' said Bella, blushing.

May had done a good job of protecting Bella's honour, or so she thought, but soon she and Vance would be married, and he would never have to leave again.

She became more serious. 'It is over, isn't it, May?'

'Well, young Tom was last seen on a stagecoach heading east. We won't see him ever again. And Griffiths is up country, making life miserable for some other poor varmints.'

'But we know he was behind this. I can't help wondering what he has in store for us next. I don't believe he'd give up this easily.'

'Well, maybe he won't. But he ain't gonna come sniffing around here when you and Vance are married. He knew your brother was weak, and he probably thought you would be too, being a woman all on your own. But he knows Vance isn't. I don't think he'll try to take on your man.'

'He tried to have him killed.'

'Yes, but things are different now. Unlike those other two no-good marshals, Vance has the respect of the community. The people who were scared of Griffiths before aren't as scared of him now. They're not going to stand by and see their marshal killed.'

Bella wondered if that were true. In their private moments together, she knew that Vance still thought he was only in Milton on sufferance.

'I worry about you too,' he had told her the night before. Bella was sitting on his knee in the parlour, running her fingers through his hair, whilst his hands playfully caressed the bodice of her dress.

May bustled around noisily in the kitchen so that they would know she was listening out for any impropriety.

'Me? Why, darling?' She leaned in and kissed his lips tenderly.

'I was thinking about my great-grandmother, and how she cut and run.'

'I'm not the cut and running type,' said Bella.

'You were going to go home to England.'

'Only because I thought you were in love with someone else. Vance, my love, I'll never leave you.'

'What about when we have children?' His hands slid up her bodice, as the merest suggestion of children had put other thoughts into his mind. 'You know when my father said we should be proud of our heritage, I don't think he realised what it would cost us. Cost me. I grew up being called a half-breed. I don't want that for my kids.'

'Are you saying you've changed your mind?' asked Bella, feeling panic rising in her throat.

'No. I love you, and I don't ever want to let you go.' He pulled her closer still. 'But I don't want to lose you either, when we have children and they have to

166

suffer the same insults I did.'

'I'm not going anywhere, darling. We're going to have wonderful children and bring them up to know they're as good as everyone else. All children are made fun of at school for something or other. What matters is that they've got parents at home who love them and help them through it. That's what we'll do. Together.'

She kissed him again, their kiss becoming deeper and hotter.

'I want you so much,' he whispered to her. 'I don't know how much longer I can wait for you, Bella. I need to be able to touch you. To finish what we started in the cave that morning.'

'I know, darling. I feel the same way.'

'Tomorrow we'll go to Milton and make arrangements for the wedding.'

'Yes, but,' Bella dropped her voice a little lower, 'tonight, after May sends you home, I could come out and meet you in the vineyard.'

'You're a wanton woman, Bella Tennyson,' he said, smiling dreamily.

'That's how being with you makes me feel.' She slipped her fingers inside his shirt, and rested her head on his shoulder. 'So?'

'I told you that the next time you touched a man like that you'd better be willing to deal with the consequences.'

'I know,' murmured Bella, brushing her mouth against his between words. 'I . . . remember . . . every . . . single . . . word.'

★ ★ ★

'What are you smiling at?' asked May as they stood on the porch the next morning.

'Oh, nothing,' said Bella. 'Vance! I'm ready when you are.'

'It's a funny thing,' said May as Vance put on his shirt and started walking towards them. 'But last night I thought I heard a prowler again.'

'Did you?'

'Yes, but when I looked out I thought I saw you.'

'Oh.'

'You were probably sleepwalking.'

'Yes, that's probably it,' said Bella.

'Not that I've ever known you sleepwalk before.'

Vance drew nearer to the porch.

'Mind you,' May continued. 'You'd think all these rocks under a person's feet would wake them up.'

'Wake who up?' Vance raised an eyebrow.

'May thought she saw me sleepwalking last night,' Bella explained.

'Really?'

'I don't have to get my shotgun, do I, marshal?' asked May. She was grinning but her eyes were steely. 'You're gonna make an honest woman of my little girl without a rifle in your back, aren't you?'

'I most certainly am, Miss Tucker.'

'That's okay then. But,' she turned to Bella, 'there's to be no more . . . sleepwalking . . . till we get you down that aisle, do you hear? I'll get Shen or one of the boys to sit out on the porch all night if I have to.'

'Like I said,' Vance said to Bella as they walked to the buggy, 'the sooner we get married the better.'

'But,' murmured Bella, 'it's a long way to Milton and we'll be alone.'

May called out from the porch, 'Vance! Bella! Shen said he has to go into Milton. Wait on him a while. You can give him a lift. In fact, now I think on it, I've got things to do down there. I'll come along myself.'

'It was a nice idea while it lasted,' said Vance, laughing, as he helped Bella up onto the front seat of the buggy. 'But they won't always be around, will they?'

'We will until you put a ring on that girl's finger,' said May, slapping him firmly on the shoulder and climbing into the back of the buggy.

'Miss Tucker, do you have Indian blood in you? Because I've never known a white woman who could creep up on someone like that before.' Vance climbed into his own seat. Bella placed her hand on his thigh.

'No, my family were of German

stock. But I've learned a lot from watching you over the past week.' May removed Bella's hand from Vance's leg. 'That's enough of that. Shen's an old man and set in his ways.'

'You don't need your rifle now, Miss Tucker,' said Vance, looking back at the gun May held in her hand.

'I'm taking it to get a new firing pin. So you're safe — at least until we get to Milton.'

* * *

Milton was bustling when they arrived. More settlers came every day. Families and children filled the streets.

'I ought to send a telegram to my father again,' said Vance as he guided the buggy into a space outside the hardware store. 'These people will be needing homes, and he might be able to help out.'

'It was good of him to offer to help us restock the vineyard,' said May, as she clambered out of the back.

'He likes the idea of wine-growing,' said Vance. 'It appeals to his more cultured side.' He looked to Bella. 'He's also hoping you'll save me from this awful life of crime I lead.'

'I don't want to change you one bit,' said Bella. 'Shen, do you think you'll hear something today?'

Shen was at Bella's side, ready to help her down. 'I hope so, Miss Bella. The lawyer said he would try to rush things through.'

'Good luck,' she said, when she was safely on the ground. 'If you have any problems, we'll be over at the church, seeing the preacher.'

'I wouldn't want to disturb you when you have such important business to take care of,' he said, smiling kindly. 'I will wait until you are finished.'

'Very well. We'll see you both in a little while.'

Bella and Vance waved to May and Shen and headed for the church.

Half an hour later, they were coming back out again and shaking hands with the preacher, when they saw Griffiths standing at the end of the main road. He was about two hundred yards away from them.

'Marshal Eagleson,' said Griffiths. He swayed on his feet. 'Marshal! You come here and fight like a man.'

Others on the street had stopped to watch him. Bella saw Shen in the background, and was perplexed when he turned and ran in the opposite direction. Was he abandoning them to their fate?

'Bella, go back inside with the preacher,' said Vance.

'Vance . . . '

'Please, darling. Do as I say. What do you want Mister Griffiths?'

'I want to finish what others couldn't. Tom has run away, and Bill is dead. The others who work for me, they've got weak. They're more scared of you than they are of me. They think you're some kind of ghost.' Griffiths spat on the ground. 'They've created a mythology about you. The Indian marshal who disappears into the darkness.'

'Bella, for goodness' sake, go inside.'

'I'm not leaving you.'

'I'm going to kill you, marshal,' Griffiths said. His hand was on his gun belt, but he had not yet drawn. He was too far away from them to be any real threat. 'This is my town, and I don't want you in it. You or that little Indian loving trollop.'

Bella heard Vance's sharp intake of breath and saw his hand snap towards his own gun.

'No,' she whispered urgently. 'What he says means nothing, Vance. It's about him and the sort of man he is. It's not about me.'

'She's right, marshal,' said the preacher, who was standing on Vance's other side. 'Don't commit a mortal sin over something you know isn't true.'

'I'm the marshal here,' said Vance in a low growl. 'It's my job to uphold the law, and he's breaking it by threatening me and another citizen.'

'You can justify that to yourself all

you want, Vance,' said the preacher. 'But we'll all know it's because of what he's just said about Bella. Besides, I know you're a good shot, but you'd never hit him from here.'

'I'll get a little closer then,' said Vance.

'No,' said Bella. 'He might kill you.'

Griffiths was moving closer all the time. He would soon be within firing distance of them.

'Mister Griffiths,' said Bella. 'Let's talk about this. About the vineyard.'

'Bella, no,' Vance hissed.

'You were right, you know. My brother misled you, and he shouldn't have. Perhaps we can talk about it. Of course, I can't let you have it as part of the bet, but you were going to make me an offer.'

'Bella, what are you doing?'

'I'm saving your life.'

'Darling, he's not going to kill me.'

'You're too late. I don't want it. With the damage from the fire, it'll cost me too much to make it viable. It's damaged goods now. Much like you, Miss Tennyson.'

'That's Mrs Eagleson to you,' said Vance. 'And if you say one more insulting thing about my wife, I will kill you where you stand.'

'You're not married yet,' said Griffiths.

'Yes they are,' said the preacher. His brow was awash with sweat. 'I just performed the ceremony myself, with my wife and daughter as witnesses. Marshal, I urge you to rethink. I understand you feel the need to protect your wife's honour, but don't let your marriage start like this. You can take him, you know you can. Even if he wasn't as drunk as a skunk. In which case it's little more than murder.'

'If he doesn't kill me, I'm going to kill him,' said Griffiths. 'I will show people who's really in charge of this town.'

'I don't think so, Griffiths.'

Bella looked around to see where the new voice came from. It was Ike Peterson. He had several of his men with him. She looked to the other side of the street and saw Mr Grant and his men. There must have been about twenty of them in all. Whilst Griffiths had been talking, they had moved in closer. Her heart swelled when she saw Shen standing shoulder to shoulder with Mr Peterson.

'Keep out of this, Ike,' said Griffiths, 'if you know what's good for you.'

'It's not about what's good for me, Griffiths. It's about what's good for Milton. And we've decided you're not. The marshal on the other hand, is. There's less killing goes on around here, apart from the poor English boy, and there's less dishonesty in the officers of the law. Milton is starting to turn into the sort of place people want to settle, have families. We kinda like that. It'll bring business and prosperity to the town and we'll all benefit. But you, Griffiths, you're staining the place with your presence.'

'I have Milton's best interests at heart,' said Griffiths.

'No, you don't. You might have, when you first started out here, but the only person you're interested in now is yourself. We want you to leave.'

'I will, but not before I kill that half-breed.'

'You shoot the marshal,' said Mr Grant, on the other side of the street, 'and five seconds later you'll have nineteen, maybe twenty bullets making holes in you. Go on, Griffiths. Do it, so we can use you as an example to any other upstart who wants to come here thinking he can run the town and make us pay for water rights.'

'That's what this is all about,' said Griffiths. 'You don't care about the marshal, or Milton, you only want your cattle to graze. Well, fair enough. We can do a deal.'

'No deal,' said Peterson. 'You seem to have missed a major point. We like the marshal and we like his little bride there. They're good people and better for this town than you've ever been.'

Vance's hand had relaxed on his gun,

and he took hold of Bella's hand. Pride welled up inside her.

Griffiths looked at his own gun, and then at all the guns pointing at him. Even from a distance, Bella could feel turmoil emanating from him. He definitely wanted Vance dead, but his own survival instinct was stronger.

But for how long, she wondered. How long before he turned up again?

'Okay, I'll leave,' said Griffiths. 'I've got new interests up country now. Milton is finished for me. Especially now it embraces half-breeds and their . . . ' He uttered a word that made the bystanders gasp.

'Let it go,' whispered Bella, feeling Vance's hand tense in hers. 'Darling, please let it go. They're all on our side. Don't you see?'

'Yes, I see,' said Vance, his voice sounding thick with emotion. He put his arm around Bella and kissed her.

Griffiths dropped his hand to his side, and the tension visibly loosened. The other men dropped their own guns, putting them back in their holsters. Griffiths half-turned, as if to leave, then spun around, with his gun raised and pointed at Vance and Bella. There was a loud retort, but Griffiths was dead before he fired the shot.

Vance and Bella walked from the church to where his body lay on the ground. Others crowded around to see the scene.

'It's a good job one of us still had our gun out,' said May, coming out of a side road with her rifle aloft. She joined the small group at the centre of the larger circle. 'That's for Andrew and Bill,' she said, looking down at Griffiths' body. 'They might have been a bad lot, but they were family. Are you gonna arrest me, marshal?'

'No, I'm not Miss Tucker. You might have just shot a man, but you did it to save our lives. Besides, you're family.' Vance looked around the other citizens for confirmation.

'That's right,' said Ike Peterson. 'She's one of us. There's so many folk out on the street today, all with their guns out, it's hard to tell who fired the shot that killed him. Don't you agree, Grant?'

Mr Grant nodded. 'Yep.'

Ike Peterson turned to Shen and shook his hand. 'Thanks for coming to fetch us, Shen. You need any help bringing that good lady of yours over from China, you give me a holler. My brother works in the state department. Now, we'd best leave these young people to start their married life. Go on, marshal. The deputies can sort this out. Mind you, I've got a bone to pick with you both about missing out on a party.'

'We'll have a wedding party soon,' Bella promised.

'Glad to hear it. Now, go home the two of you and be happy.'

★ ★ ★

Bella stood on the porch, watching the sun set in the west. If she squinted, she could just about miss out the burned part of the vineyard. Vance came out and stood behind her, putting his arms around her waist. She leaned back against his chest, feeling the warmth of his body.

'No need for sleepwalking tonight, my darling,' he whispered in her ear and laughed softly.

'Pity, I rather enjoyed it.'

'Yes, me too. You're very active when you're asleep.'

'Hmm, I'm not sure what to say about you, taking advantage of a sleeping woman.'

He kissed her neck passionately, and she felt the flames of the night before ignite again.

'Is May alright?' asked Bella. 'She seemed a bit down this evening. I wonder if she's upset that we got married without her being there.'

'She's just lost her brother, and then killed a man. She would be inhuman if it didn't get to her on some level. She's a strong woman, though. She'll work her way through it.'

'With our help.'

'Yes. With our help. She's gone to bed now.'

'May said that we have to climb the mountains, not stride over them. But that we all need a helping hand.'

'She's right, most of the time. But I reckon that at this moment, the way I feel with you in my arms, I could step right on over them.'

Bella turned to face him, and stroked his cheek with her hand. 'I love you so much, my darling.'

'I love you too.'

'It's really over now, isn't it?' she asked.

'No.'

'No?'

'For us this is just the beginning.' Vance kissed her, then picked her up and stepped right on over the mountain.

When Elizabeth's grandfather died, there was no sign of a will; and, devastatingly, she discovered she was now dependent on his heir. When the new Lord and Lady Hartford and their twin daughters arrived, they reduced her status to that of a servant. Elizabeth is determined to leave Hartford Hall in the New Year and find work as a governess. But the arrival of Sir James Worthington to make an offer for Lady Eleanor only adds to her difficulties . . .

ABIGAIL MOOR: THE DARKEST DAWN

Valerie Holmes

Miss Abigail Hammond grows up in Beckton Manor as the adopted daughter of Lord Hammond. However, when he falls terminally ill, her life, her identity and her safety are all threatened. Then, faced with being forced into a marriage to a man she loathes, she runs away with her maid on Lord Hammond's instructions. Abigail tries to discover the truth of her past, despite her efforts being constantly foiled by her life-long maid, Martha.